# The Waiting Place

# The Waiting Place

## Sharron Arksey

TURNSTONE PRESS

The Waiting Place
copyright © Sharron Arksey 2016

Turnstone Press
Artspace Building
206-100 Arthur Street
Winnipeg, MB
R3B 1H3 Canada
www.TurnstonePress.com

Turnstone Press gratefully acknowledges the assistance of the Canada Council for the Arts, the Manitoba Arts Council, the Government of Canada through the Canada Book Fund, and the Province of Manitoba through the Book Publishing Tax Credit and the Book Publisher Marketing Assistance Program.

Printed and bound in Canada by Friesens for Turnstone Press.

Library and Archives Canada Cataloguing in Publication

Arksey, Sharron, author
    The waiting place / Sharron Arksey.

Issued in print and electronic formats.
ISBN 978-0-88801-591-4 (paperback).--ISBN 978-0-88801-592-1 (epub).--
ISBN 978-0-88801-593-8 (mobipocket).--ISBN 978-0-88801-594-5 (pdf)

    I. Title.

PS8601.R49W35 2016          C813'6          C2016-902823-2
                                            C2016-902824-0

*For Erwin*

# The Waiting Place

# ONE

*My name is Susan, but my husband calls me Sus. It rhymes with "shoes" which I haven't been able to get my swollen feet into for the past two weeks. Or "snooze" which sounds like a good idea but I don't think is possible. Or "booze" which sounds even better but has been off the menu for the past nine months.*

*Most people call me Susan, although Dad, when he wants to torment me, has occasionally called me Susie. Wake up little Susie. Susie Q. Right now I would answer to any name that would get me out of this hospital. Any second now my body is going to be ripped apart by a tsunami that will swell and swell and swell until I want to scream and curse and swear. I am only two centimetres dilated. Two centimetres is about the size of a postage stamp. I would like to cancel this stamp.*

The contractions began shortly after lunch. The first one made my knees buckle. I was holding onto the kitchen counter with both hands when the phone rang. Because our house is a dead zone for cell service, Glen had called our landline and it was an effort to get from the counter to the wall where the phone was mounted.

"Sus, can you do me a favour?"

My husband had gone out after lunch to repair pasture fences, a typical job for late April. But when he got there, he realized he had left his work gloves on the porch. He wanted me to run them down to him.

"Can't," I said. "I think you need to do me a favour instead."

"What?" he asked.

"Get me to the hospital."

He took longer than should have been necessary to drive the four miles between pasture and farmyard. I timed his travel time with my contractions. He arrived with a handful of crocuses.

"I stopped to pick these," he said. "Thought you might like them."

I might have liked them better if you got here ten minutes earlier, I thought but didn't say. I showed admirable restraint, if I do say so myself.

Glen brings me crocuses every spring. I prefer them to roses or any of the flowers you purchase in a store, which is good because Glen has never bought me roses and I would be surprised if he ever did. But he always makes a point of stopping to pick a bouquet of wild flowers. Crocuses grow early in the spring before other plants have dared to break the crust on frozen soil. Yet they feel so soft and their colour is a gentle pastel mauve. Softness and strength in one small plant, an antonym of itself.

At that moment, however, I wasn't appreciative. Another contraction had started and I let out a groan. Glen hurriedly put the flowers on the kitchen table and helped me out to the car. Once he had me settled in the car, he went back to the house to get my bag and then finally we were on our way.

The doctor wasn't sure I was in labour. But since we live more than an hour away from the hospital, he admitted me to be on the safe side. He was not my regular doctor; Dr. Thomas had chosen this inopportune time to go on vacation. I wanted Dr. Thomas with her femaleness. Is that a word? If it isn't, it should be.

"Am I in labour?" I asked the nurse who was middle-aged and comfortably rounded.

"Oh, I think so."

Always ask the nurse. No offence, Doc, but I'm going to take her word over yours.

Just then my water broke, soaking the sheet beneath me.

"I think so, too," I said.

That's when my husband took his departure.

"I'm gonna go pick up some more staple nails," Glen said. "It won't take long and you're not going anywhere."

"Funny man," the nurse said as she expertly removed the wet sheet from underneath me.

"Farmer man," I said.

"Ah," she said. "Never come to town without a list of things to pick up. If you have to take the time and use the money up on the gas, you have to make it worth your while."

"You must be married to one, too," I said.

"You bet."

"Might as well kill two birds with one stone even if your wife is in labour at the hospital." I could even joke about it.

"Especially if your wife is in labour at the hospital, in some cases I've seen," she replied.

When she turned to leave, I wanted to hang onto her with both arms. Stay with me, please. I want your wisdom and your experience and your sense of humour right here in the room with me. Another contraction was tearing me apart.

# TWO

*In prenatal classes, they taught us to focus on something to take our minds off the pain: a light fixture, a crack in the wall, a ceiling tile. My name seems like a good choice. The contractions are taking me to a place where I am nameless. It is the pain I would like to forget. So I focus on my name. I was named after my dad's mother and I grew up wishing that my grandmother had a different name. Susanne perhaps or Suzanne with a "z" for a more exotic touch. Susanna even. Or Susana which has a Spanish feel with a hint of castanets in the background.*

*Oh Susana, don't you cry for me.*

*Tomorrow this'll all be over.*

*I'm on my way to*

*Centimetre number three.*

*I'm a poet.*

*Or I could think about things that come in twos. Like*

*two hands, two feet, two ears, two eyes, two arms, two legs. Husband and wife. Father and mother. Grandparents. Left feet if you're a bad dancer. Socks. Gloves like the ones Glen forgot today. Two timer. It's a thin slice that doesn't have two sides. Two's company. Two wrongs don't make a right. The beast with two backs. Twins. No. Do not go there.*

I got pregnant the day that we moved our bulls home from pasture.

It's true. We spent a sunny Saturday afternoon in late July hauling our bulls out of their respective pastures. Then that night we made a baby. In a weird sort of way, it seems appropriate. There had to be a bull at home to get the job done.

The bulls weren't coming home to have sex, mind you. They were getting a vacation. Enforced celibacy. No conjugal relations for them for months and months, until the members of their harem gave birth and it was time for another go round. Being a bull is not a hard life, although protecting your territory can be brutal, I suppose. And being male is no guarantee that you get to be a bull, so just avoiding castration is a milestone worth celebrating.

Generally speaking, our bulls are a quiet and well-behaved bunch. We drove to each of the four pastures, separated the bull from its herd and walked him towards the stock trailer. At home we unloaded them into an enclosed space behind the barns. The youngest animal had grown cocky over the summer but a swift bunt from the elder statesman of the herd put it in its place, at least temporarily. We knew the fighting would continue for a couple of days until the social hierarchy had been re-established and the dominant male proclaimed.

After supper, we went for a drive to all the pastures, more for the drive itself than for any real need to check the cattle, which we had seen just hours before. Once we had turned onto a gravel road, I slipped off my seat belt and moved illegally towards the centre of the front seat. Bucket seats were not an option when this old truck was made. Glen put a tanned arm around me and I snuggled against him.

I didn't feel much like snuggling later that night. The mattress we sleep on is an old one that slopes downward towards the centre from both sides; I call it our marriage bed because of the intimacy the mattress demands. We don't have air conditioning and our bedroom was stifling. We had positioned a fan so that the moving air brought some relief, but not enough. When Glen cupped one breast, I resisted.

"It's too hot," I said.

"It's going to get hotter," he said and lowered his mouth to my nipple.

Afterwards the thought did cross my mind that the timing was just about perfect for making a baby. Mom tells a story about a cousin of hers who had sex with her boyfriend right in the middle of her menstrual cycle.

"That's the safe time, right?" she asked my mother. They were and still are best friends.

"You have it backwards," Mom said. "The safe times are at the beginning and end of your cycle. The middle is not safe." Sure enough, Mom's cousin was pregnant and that was back in the days when an unexpected pregnancy

9

meant an unexpected wedding, too. I think Mom told me the story as an object lesson. Middle of the road is not always the best answer.

"Mom, I know that," I told her.

I didn't, not really, but I was a teenager. I knew everything.

So when my period didn't arrive on schedule last summer, I wasn't surprised and the home pregnancy test I picked up in town confirmed my suspicions. I came out of the bathroom brandishing the test strip and Glen understood immediately.

We'd been married for three years and we both wanted children or at least we said we did. The precautions we took were slapdash. Sometimes we took them, sometimes we didn't.

Still when it happened, we were shell-shocked. Glen worried about the money angle. Could we afford a child? We were making payments to his parents for the farm and to the bank for equipment and operating costs. Cattle prices are finally beginning to rebound after the BSE crisis in 2003, but we live in fear that the disease will resurface and we'll have to go through it over again. Mad Cow Disease spawned many cartoons of cows with their tongues lolling outside their mouths and eyes freakishly staring out the sides of their heads. I thought it unfair to make a comic strip out of their suffering and eventual death. If they didn't die from the disease itself, they were destroyed and their carcasses tossed on a funeral pyre in the name of public safety.

My parents and Glen's got through it. But they were

established farmers; they didn't have the debts that Glen and I started out with.

Our grain crops had been all right last year, but not excellent, and this year's crops were still a long way from the bins. A crop might look good in the field, but you never feel confident until the harvest is completed. So much can happen in between: no rain, too much rain, an early frost, an insect infestation, plant disease.

Me, I wondered what kind of mother I would make. What if I wasn't a good one? What if I screwed it up? I have some experience at being an aunt and I think I play that role quite well, but being a parent is something else. You don't get to send the child home.

The absence of a period is not something one can be indifferent to; it either makes one happy or scared, sometimes both at the same time. I suppose the same could be said about a period's arrival. It depends on whether or not pregnancy is a goal. It had always been good news when my period arrived, even though it seemed unfair that good news came with cramps and inconvenience. But unfair would have been an understatement if the cramps and inconvenience of a period were bad news, not good.


When I was still living at home and Dad told me to do something, I always did what he asked.

Not that I did it that very second. I usually waited until the TV commercial or until I got off the phone. But I tried to get started before he told me a second time.

I have never been afraid of my dad. He's pretty tame, really—Dad never spanked any of us kids when we were little, and he belonged to the last generation, which accepted spanking as a normal part of parental discipline. So I was never worried about any physical repercussions. But if any of us didn't do as he said, or if we procrastinated even just a little, we got "the question."

"Do you know what your grandfather would say?"

The answer varied, since Grandpa had a vast repertoire of quotable quotes and memorable reactions. It might be, "If I had said no when Grandpa asked me to do something, my ass would have been so sore I couldn't have sat down for a month of Sundays. I learned real quick."

"When your grandpa said, 'Jump', I said, 'How high?'"

Another one of Grandpa's lines was "If you fly with the crows, you're gonna get shot." Dad used that one the time my older brother Jonathan and his friends got caught with open liquor in the car. Grandpa also said that "the poorer the Indian, the more dogs he has."

When Dad asked the question, my brothers and I would always chime in with the answer that fit. It was funny at first, but it got old quickly. I got the feeling that Mom didn't appreciate the question that much either. She usually didn't say anything, just continued on with whatever she was doing. But one time I heard her tell Dad, "Dave, let's make our own rules. We don't have to live by your father's."

Anyway, I did whatever Dad wanted, just to save time.

One evening he wanted me to take out a salt lick to the heifers in the home pasture. I said, "Sure, Dad" and headed out to the machine shed to get the ATV. The only detour I took was a short one to get my cell from the bedroom.

I drove the ATV out to the shed and loaded a salt block onto the back. Then I set out down the gravel road to the pasture.

The tiger lilies were out, I noticed, and thought about picking some when I returned later. They would look nice on the kitchen table.

I turned off at the entrance to the pasture and drove to where the depleted salt lick was.

Once I had put down the new salt, I got back on the ATV and pulled out the cell. A quick glance showed me what I had suspected. No signal. So I started driving around the pasture, holding up the phone every once in a while to check for service. I knew it was there somewhere.

When I found it, I stopped the ATV and texted, "Call me."

Then I settled down to wait, watching the heifers approach the salt lick. There were also a few cows with calves in the pasture because Dad said that heifers were knot heads and they need the older cows there as role models. Heifers have a lot to learn.

There was one bull out there too, a bull specially selected to mate with young heifers. I didn't see him now and assumed he was in the bush somewhere resting from his labours. I wasn't worried. Some bulls you need to watch out for, but not this one. He was a pet. Well, as much a pet as any bull can be.

My border collie Tigger was a black and white streak coming towards me from the gate. He hadn't been around when I left the yard, but must have seen me leave. I know that Tigger is a cat's name, well, a tiger's name really, but the pup was so bouncy, I didn't think I had a choice.

The dog's approach broke up the ring of heifers surrounding the salt lick. I started picking them out by name. There was Diana and Sarah, Beatrice and Eugenie, Princess

and Duchess. The year before we had been big into royalty.
Dad said that it was good that we named our animals.

"This is a family farm, after all," he said.

My phone rang.

"It's all good," I said, dispensing with any other greeting.

"Really?" Tyler asked.

"Yes, really."

I had got my period that morning, after five days of
waiting. Tyler and I had been dating for about a year. We
had known each other since we were little kids, the way
you know everyone in a farming community. But we were
just friends. When he needed a date for grad the year
before, he asked me. We'd been dating ever since and we
were obviously past the "just friends" stage.

We were good about the condom thing, but I knew they
weren't perfect. When my period was late, I right away
thought about defective condoms. It had to be something
like that because as my grandpa always said, "It was no
virgin birth."

"Well, that's good," Tyler said once he'd deciphered my
code.

"That's what I said."

"No more worries then. Hey, Susan?"

"Yeah?"

"I was wondering. We have a ball game Friday night
and the guys are planning a trip to the bar afterwards. I
wasn't gonna go, but now with you being out of commission and all ..."

I didn't say anything, not at first. Tyler was nineteen to
my seventeen. Going to the bar with him was one thing I
could not do, at least not legally. And going out with the

guys for a beer or two or three after a ball game was fine with me, really. It was the "out of commission" thing that threw me.

"Susan?"

"Piss off," I said.

"Did I say something wrong?"

"Never mind," I said. Oh, what the hell, tell him. "I guess if you can't have sex with me, there's no point in going out with me."

"Fuck, Susan, you know I didn't mean that."

"What did you mean then?"

"Well, you know ..."

"No, really I don't know, Ty."

"Susan, I don't get it. Is this some hormone thing?"

Talk about setting a match to a smoldering flame. Hormone thing? For five days I had waited for the period to end all sentences, and when it finally arrived, I was suddenly out of commission and my feelings reduced to a hormone thing. We could talk; that would be cool. We could go to a movie, go for a drive. We could kiss. I was no stranger to hand jobs. Sex is more than in and out and penetration during a period was not unheard of, although personally I thought it sounded rather messy. At least it would be safe. Had I suddenly become untouchable because I had my period? No wonder the world was screwed up, if that's the way people thought.

There I was believing that we had an excuse to celebrate. Instead Ty figured it was an excuse to stay away. And he did it with such speed that he must have had it planned all along. What if the news had not been good?

"Forget it," I said. "Go with the guys."

"You sure?"

Idiot.

"Yes, I'm sure. Talk to you tomorrow."

"Yeah. Susan? I'm glad you're out of commission."

How's a person supposed to respond to that?

"Me too."

I ended the call and stuck the phone back in my pocket.

"Tigger," I said, scratching the dog behind its ears, "maybe you can tell me. Are all guys assholes?"

Tigger rolled over onto his back, exposing his belly and begging for a rub. I obliged.

"Are you telling me what I think you're telling me?" I asked. Tigger closed his eyes. "I thought so, you fickle dog," I said. "You'd roll over for anyone willing to pat you, wouldn't you?"

I walked over to where Duchess was grazing. Duchess was my favourite of that year's heifer crop. She was a deep red colour with a white blaze on her forehead.

"Hi, girl," I said, giving her a pat on the neck. "Sorry, I forgot the brush."

Often when I went out to see the cattle, I brought the cattle brush and spent time grooming their hides. They liked it. But I'd had other things on my mind that evening and never thought of it.

I hoped Duchess wouldn't have a hard time with her first calf. A farmer did the best he could, breeding her to a small bull with proven genetics to suggest low birth weights for the calves. But nothing was for certain. The calf could be a throwback to some larger animal way back in the gene pool.

Sometimes even calves less than a year old can get bred

in summer pasture. Dad always took the bulls out early, but there was a time one of the younger heifers ended up in calf. The calf was born dead and the heifer died, too.

I thought about going back home for the brush, but decided against it. Instead I gave Duchess one last pat and started up the ATV.

The tiger lilies in the ditch were a deep red-orange, their stamens sticky with pollen. I brought one up to smell and rubbed my nose afterwards, certain that there would be pollen residue there. I picked about a dozen of the wild flowers, careful to break the stem rather than pull the plant out by the roots as Dad had taught me.

I wasn't really mad at Ty, I realized. I had been, but it had worn off quickly. What was it Mom said? He's a man; he can't help it. Maybe it was just that easy. And I wasn't pregnant, so it didn't have to be any harder.

I wasn't sure how Mom would have reacted if my period had never arrived. I thought that she would have gone quiet and inside herself but Mom could be all over the map sometimes. She might have burst into tears. Eventually, she would have come to me with a plan for how to get through this. I just didn't know what would have come first, the fire or the ice.

But Dad? That was a no brainer.

My very first thought when I woke that morning and saw that my period had started was, "I don't have to tell Mom and Dad." My second thought was, "I have to tell Ty."

Tyler and I continued dating for several months, but it was nowhere near as hot and heavy as it had been. By the start of my Grade Twelve year, we had pretty much called it quits and by the time I graduated the next June, I was dating someone else.

I occasionally run into Tyler since we both live in the community. He and his wife have two children with a third on the way. I often wonder if being out of commission also applied to being pregnant. I personally would not like that, but perhaps Ty's wife learned to appreciate it.

Since Grandpa died, Dad has voiced the question less and less, but lately he's been coming out with some of his own malapropisms. We tell him he's becoming more and more like his dad. Same genes, different pocket.

Glen and I decided not to tell anyone about my pregnancy for the first few months in case there were problems. A woman we knew had told everyone within telling distance when her pregnancy test came back positive. She miscarried a month later. When I stopped to think about it though, I wondered how it started, this reticence to talk about pregnancy until it is well on its way. Was it a kind of superstition? What would be wrong with letting others share in my initial happiness so that, if there were a miscarriage, they could share in my grief as well?

Of course, the secret was ours alone only for the time it took for me to see my family doctor. Once the pregnancy was officially confirmed, the clinic staff were also in on the secret.

I did have a hard time not telling Mom. I wondered whether she would suss it out for herself, see something in my face or in the size of my boobs which had suddenly become much fuller. If she did, she never said anything.

I spent the rest of the summer and most of the fall

puking my guts out. I took time off from my job at the local vet clinic to help with the harvest in late August and chewed on unsalted crackers as I sat in the grain truck and watched the combine go round and round the field. I always took a book along in the hope that I would get to read it.

But because I had to keep up with two combines, there wasn't always much time to read between loads. And once dusk fell, my job in the fields would be over for the day. I would cook the evening meal and Glen and I would eat later. Normally I loved the harvest, straw dust, late hours, and all. This year I dragged myself to bed each night, supper dishes sometimes still on the table.

Whenever I did get a chance to read in the truck, my choice was an old book of baby names that I found in one of the upstairs bedrooms in our house. We inherited the house from Glen's parents who inherited it from my father-in-law's parents. The house was originally owned by a family named Larsen who retired to the West Coast in the late 1940s.

It's one of those square brick houses with large rooms, high ceilings, and a veranda facing the front. Originally, there was a veranda on each floor, but the one at the higher level was dismantled when it became unsafe. All that remains to indicate its former existence is an upper storey door that remains locked for safety.

When Mr. and Mrs. Larsen moved away, they left an attic full of belongings they had no interest in paying haulage for to British Columbia. Glen's grandparents added to the hoard and no one ever got around to cleaning it out. I like to spend time up there, digging through old trunks. I once found a National Geographic dated June 1945 with stories on China and the liberation of Europe. I also found a copy of the 1976 Eaton's catalogue, the last ever mail-order catalogue offered by the company.

"We have history in our attic," I told Glen and he laughed at me.

"Old houses and young animals, that's my Sus," he said.

I felt like a cliché when he said that, thoughts and feelings reduced to a rehash of things thought and felt too many times before. I would prefer to be an original.

If I were an eBay person, I could perhaps make my fortune offering vintage items from our attic for sale. An intriguing thought. Still, if I ever did clean out the attic, how would I spend my spare time? And if I ever did find anything valuable up there, there would be the ethical question of which family member should reap the rewards. My in-laws might well want it for themselves and claim prior rights. Besides, I am not likely to ever get beyond the stage of thinking about an eBay enterprise. I have grand ideas, but not always the discipline to carry them through. I do love those afternoon searches, however. Each box is the promise of new treasure.

This baby book was vintage, although in far from pristine condition. Some of the pages were ripped and a young child drew pictures in red crayon in the girls' names starting with the "S" section. Doesn't matter. I learned a great deal from the book despite its condition.

"Susan," I discovered, comes from the Hebrew word for lily. Now that I hadn't known. My very prosaic name is a flower. Imagine that. I might have thought of brown-eyed Susans, I suppose, except that my eyes are blue.

"Glen" is of Irish and Gaelic origin, meaning a narrow valley between hills.

Susan and Glen together make a lily of the valley. I found that quite appealing especially considering that lilies of the valley are commonly found in bridal bouquets, but when I told Glen, he laughed. Then he reminded me that all parts of the lily of the valley plant are highly poisonous.

The book was so old that many of the baby names I had become accustomed to were not included. The names I did find were from my parents' generation: Cheryl, Donna, Karen, Linda, Patricia, and Sandra for girls; Dennis, Gary, Larry, Roger, and Mark for boys. For more modern names, I had to go to the Internet or find a newer book. When I eventually surfed the Internet, however, I discovered that my old name book had become fashionable again. Favourite girls' names in the book were Emma, Emily, Ava and Olivia. Popular boys' names included Ethan and Carter. According to the Internet, those names were once again popular.

"If it's a girl, we could name her after one of the cats," Glen said one evening as we sat eating supper.

"Which one?" I asked.

We have two indoor cats, my choice, not Glen's. One is a gray tabby and the other is orange. I named them Samantha and Tabitha after an old TV program that my parents watch on cable. Samantha is a witch who married a mortal; their daughter, who would also prove to have magical powers, is named Tabitha. But the feline Tabitha turned out to be a male and so we shortened its name to Tab. Samantha eventually became plain Sam, same as my younger brother, although having a brother and a female cat with the same name was nothing more than a coincidence.

The indoor cats are a continuous source of irritation for my mother-in-law who did not allow such a thing when this house was hers. I suspect she was as fond of the barn cats as I am, but she never welcomed them past the front step.

My mother-in-law and her in-laws lived together in this house for many years. I think that must have been difficult. Living together began as a temporary measure for them, but when Glen's grandmother was diagnosed with Parkinson's disease, the arrangement became permanent. Glen's grandmother passed away when he was eight and his grandfather when he was nineteen.

Perhaps it explains, at least partly, why Joan and Joe moved to town before we got married. There was never any suggestion that we would all live together, temporarily or otherwise.

In the case of Joan and me, the yard became our major battleground, although battleground is an exaggeration. Our skirmishes are the passive-aggressive kind, shots fired via a third person, criticism cloaked in courtesy. In Joan's tenure, the yard was a place of landscaped perfection: weeded flower beds, manicured lawns, a park outside the bedroom windows. But I am not a gardener, or at least not a very good one. I let our two dogs roll around in the flower beds. I care more about the dogs than I do the flower beds, I guess.

There are so many other things I would rather be doing than weeding flower beds. I would rather have a plot rioting with the colours of prairie wildflowers and, to Joan's dismay, I have started one.

"But they're weeds," she said when she saw the Indian paint brush and brown-eyed Susans I transplanted that summer.

"A weed is only a weed when you find it where you don't want it to be. They're prairie flowers," I said.

Soon after we were married, I dug up some yellow lady slippers I found growing along a roadside and replanted them on the north side of the house. They bloomed for me this spring. I call them wild orchids. Why not? That's what they are. Lady slippers are related to orchids, as they are also to snapdragons.

"You do realize you're doing something illegal?" Glen asked when I moved the plants from their natural habitat to our yard.

"Shhh," I said. "I won't tell if you don't."

We have found pink lady slippers in this part of the province, but they are rare and I would never attempt to transplant them anywhere else. It's one thing to dig up a few plants out of twenty found blooming in a ditch; it's another to dig up the only plant you've seen all spring. That's the point at which it becomes a crime in my books.

I can still remember the first time I ever saw a pink lady slipper because it had such a strong and unusual effect on me. My thoughts were a cross between erotic and carnal. The flower's shape reminded me of the wet and secret places in a woman's body and its pink was the bruised colour of passion.

Crocuses, on the other hand, are not sexy, but I would like to plant them in the yard if I could. So far I have never succeeded. Crocuses like sandy soil; they thrive on challenge. The soil in this yard is too heavy; it drags them down.

I suppose that if I had my own crocus patch in the yard, there would be no need for our annual forays down gravel roads and into thawing pastures to seek them out. And Glen would no longer bring me tiny purple bouquets each spring. Am I willing to forego this little pleasure every year? Well, a few hours ago I was, come to think of it. But that had nothing to do with gardening. Nothing to do with crocuses either. A lot to do with pain though.

*Focus, Susan. Gardens. Garden flowers. Prairie flowers. Weeds.*

I would also like to have a few milkweeds to attract monarch butterflies to our yard, but that's a battle I have no chance of winning. Milkweed is a noxious weed and Glen, ever the farmer, said no way. Even Dad thought it was a bad idea. The milky white sap is toxic to almost all farm animals: cattle, sheep, horses, and poultry.

Poor maligned milkweed, positioned by nature to thwart agrarian pursuits. But manna for the monarchs which feed on nothing else. They lay their eggs on the plant and the emerging caterpillars feed on it.

So, no milkweed and maybe no monarchs. But I could have my prairie flowers and if I had them, the butterflies would come.

Herbs also draw butterflies and so I introduced sage, oregano, dill, and basil to the vegetable garden. My vegetable garden tends to be as riotous as my flower gardens and, despite my best efforts, the rows are never quite as straight as they should be.

Although, come to think of it, how straight are a garden's rows supposed to be? I suspect the straightness of the rows says more about the gardener than it does about garden productivity.

"Don't hide one behind the other," Mom said when I once confessed my feelings about Joan and the yard.

"What do you mean?"

"If you want wild flowers and prairie grasses because you love them, great. If you're filling your yard with them only because they're a change from what Joan had, don't try to pretend otherwise."

My mother Sandra is big on this "be true to yourself" stuff and I understood her logic. I thought about what she said. I didn't want straight corners and manicures. I wanted less structure and more nature. Wildflowers would always be my first choice. Any effect on my mother-in-law would be a bonus.

Glen's sister Lynne once suggested that I retain the flowerbeds and garden as a kind of tribute to the work that her mother put into them. "Change them after she's gone," Lynne said. "You're disrespecting her hard work."

If I'd been thinking fast enough, I would have told Lynne that she was welcome to spend all the time she wanted at my place keeping her mother's yard immaculate.

# THREE

Now I am three centimetres dilated and I am still waiting for Glen to return from his shopping expedition. The thought crosses my mind that perhaps we could use some of those new staple nails to close me up and put an end to this. Silly thought, I know. This baby is on its way out. Three centimetres is the length of an olive, they say. Just over an inch, like the giant martini olives I had on the table at Christmas, the kind soaked in gin. Glen said they were potent. I never sampled one. No martinis, no olives. The cats seemed to like them, though. Our cats were tipsy last Christmas.

Things that come in threes. Three Billy Goats Gruff. The Three Bears. Three French hens. Three Blind Mice. Three Little Pigs. Three sheets to the wind. Three feet in a yard. Three ring circus. Three ring binders. Wheels on a tricycle. Three Wise Men. Three strikes and you're out. 3-D. Three *trimesters in a pregnancy. Three men in a tub. Three's a crowd. Leaves of three, let it be.*

In September Glen's sister Lynne told me she was having an affair.

That's not quite the way it happened, of course. My sister-in-law and I are not close. We don't tell each other secrets.

Lynne drove over late one afternoon to get some of the excess tomatoes I had offered over the weekend. She looked different. I think she had lost a little weight, although there was more to it than that. She looked freer somehow, casual and yet confident. Her edges had become soft curves. Her blonde hair had grown out a little; the new length flattered the contours of her face. I said the first thing that came into my head. I do that a lot. It usually gets me into trouble.

"You're a new woman these days. Is there a man hiding in your closet?"

I meant it as a joke. An affair? Lynne works full time and spends two hours a day getting to and from work. She has three school-age children and whatever spare time she has is spent chauffeuring those children to hockey and music lessons and maintaining that house and yard. When would she find time for another man? It must be hard enough to find time for the man she has.

Lynne looked like a deer caught in the headlights of my question. There was a silence that lasted a long time. It was as if I had accidentally opened a door to the closet where the man hid and there he was in full frontal view. Neither Lynne nor I could pretend we hadn't seen him.

"We found each other on the Internet," she told me. Beats searching for baby names, I supposed.

"It started out just a bit of a lark," she said. "I wasn't going to meet him. Then I thought maybe I would meet him. And then I did."

Turns out they had been seeing each other in the city for the past six months. They spent time together in her hotel room when the accountant's firm where she worked sent her on training courses or to meetings. This past summer they had been going on a lot of outdoor picnics, and once, when it rained, they made use of his car.

It occurred to me that this man didn't seem willing to rent his own hotel room or meet her in a town a little closer.

"Well, it's hard for him," Lynne said. "He's married."

"Ah," I said. "Well, the breeze blows both ways on that one, doesn't it?"

"Don't be mean, Susan. He is so good in bed, you wouldn't believe it."

Well, yes, I would. I have had an experience or two with men who were really good in bed. They were just really bad out of it. I've also had an experience or two with men who failed on both counts. Lynne seemed to have hit the jackpot.

"I don't know where it's going," Lynne told me. "I don't care where it's going. It's wonderful and I'm going to enjoy it as long as it lasts."

"Be careful," I said.

"Of course," she said.

Being careful in the first place might have prevented this scenario, I thought, but didn't say. Truth is, I didn't have any kind of moral authority there. Being careful isn't who I am.

But I have never known Lynne not to be careful. Careful and cautious and constantly correct. Prissy even. If I didn't know that she and her husband Brian had children, I would never have believed her capable of something as messy as sex and childbirth.

She did have children though—three of them—Alicia, Alleyne and Adam—the Triple A batteries that kept going and going and going. She spat them out one every two years like clockwork. I think they came fully toilet trained.

"You won't tell anyone, will you?" she asked.

"No, I won't tell anyone," I said.

"Not even Glen?"

"Especially not your brother."

I was still outside in the garden when Glen came home for supper. It was one of those September evenings when everything is suffused with colour and the air is warm against your skin. I was picking tomatoes with plans to make a batch of salsa after work the following day. I had canned tomatoes and tomato juice, I had made chili sauce and spaghetti sauce, and now salsa. I had offered tomatoes to everyone I knew. When the first frost came, I wasn't sure I would try to save the ones still remaining.

"What did my sister want?" Glen asked, picking a ripe tomato from the plant nearest him and tossing it into the box between the plants.

"The tomatoes I offered her last weekend," I said.

"Right," he said, picking up a full box and heading to the house with it.

Later that evening, after Glen had fallen asleep, I sat on

the couch with the laptop and searched Internet dating sites. There seemed to be more men than women looking. I confess I had been on some of the sites before. Glen and I had done some looking together, a way to waste time on a night when there was nothing on TV. We laughed at the lines that people used to attract readers to their profile.

"Do you know how to please a woman?" I asked my husband.

"More than he does," he answered, pointing to Woman Pleaser's profile on the screen.

"Show me," I said, standing up and pulling my sweat-shirt over my head.

"I think you want it."

"Then I'll be that much easier to please, won't I?"

We had sex on the office floor that night and then again on the bed upstairs. Not what you would call romantic sex. More like rigorous calisthenics, good-for-what-ails-you exercise.

But after Lynne's revelation, I wasn't looking for titil-lation or an excuse to wake up my husband with kinky offers. I was reading the profiles and searching for hidden meanings. There are a lot of lonely people out there. It sur-prised me that Lynne was one of them.

My parents always said that you never know what goes on within the walls of a home. Taking things at face value can be a mistake. I guess they were right.

I had promised Lynn confidentiality and I intended to keep that promise. Although the thought of knocking her off her pedestal with my friends was tempting, I knew that it would not be wise. The community is too small.

# FOUR

*A camera lens is approximately four centimetres in diameter. I am a talking camera lens. I have been reduced to my baby-making parts. I have been turned inside out and pulled through the lens of my contractions.*

*Things that come in fours: Four leaf clovers. The seasons: spring, summer, fall, and winter. Directions: north, south, east, and west. Tires on a car. Legs on a chair. Legs on a cow. Stomachs in a cow. Letters in a four letter word. The four horsemen of the apocalypse. Sides to a square. Four gospels in the Bible: Matthew, Mark, Luke, and John. Playing card suits: aces, hearts, diamonds, spades.*

We weaned the calves at the beginning of October and for several days afterward the noise level outside our windows was ear-splitting. That's an exaggeration. It was not burst your eardrums loud, but it was constant and painful to hear. I always feel sorry for cows and calves alike at weaning time.

We like to get the weaning done before the weather turns. Newly-weaned calves are more susceptible and cold, wet weather often brings sickness. It is better to get the weaning process over before fall has turned to early winter. Besides, freshly-weaned calves lose weight at first and then begin to gain again once they accustom themselves to their new rations. If you wean your calves too soon before selling them, your profit margin will be smaller. Not that there's much of a profit margin in cattle. Dad used to say that, but it didn't sink in until Glen and I started farming on our own.

Glen and I watched a television documentary once about moose in Alaska. The females become mothers from hell once they are due to give birth again. They push their yearling calves away. Goodbye and good luck. Judging by the ferocity of the push, they're saying good riddance as well.

Left to themselves, cows will wean their calves naturally by refusing to let the calves suck. Eventually the calves get the message, perhaps without the stress associated with the regular weaning process that farmers use. I read somewhere that if you adopt a two-stage weaning process, the calves do better. I mentioned it to Glen, and we're looking into it. It's a matter of balancing the calves' wellbeing with farm sustainability.

We were done by about four o'clock and I made a run uptown to pick up the mail at the postal outlet in the local grocery store, as well as a quart of milk. A quick supper was on the agenda, after which Glen and I planned to take a drive back out to the pastures in case we had missed any calves. It happens.

As I reached the cemetery on my way home, I spotted Joan's car.

## ~ JOAN ~

The flowers on my parents' graves are more colourful now than they were in July. The marigolds and petunias have resisted the first frosts, adversity making them stronger, at least in the short term.

I have come to the cemetery to water the plants one more time. Soon the task will no longer be necessary. This Indian summer weather will be replaced by what I call Halloween weather: bare branches shivering in the wind. No longer a breeze. Breeze is a spring and summer word.

I refuse to pull the plants here and in the flowerbeds at home until they are well and truly frozen, when pulling them is a funeral rite rather than an act of euthanasia. I have brought my ice cream pails of water and I empty them over the plot.

Glen and Susan weaned their calves today, hauling truckload after truckload of young animals back to the yard from their summer pastures. The cows were left behind; they shall remain on pasture until there is no more grass to eat and the threat of snow is real.

I remember other such days from the past; they were long days, full of barked orders, confused activity, and occasional profanity. I was always glad we could cross that job off our list of things to do in preparation for the coming winter.

The signs are there in shortening days, coloured leaves, and the first sight of geese in the sky. And now the noise. I associate the noise with this time of year, just as I associate the smell of suddenly pungent manure with the spring thaw and the smell of freshly cut grass with summer and no smell at all with frozen winter.

The calves are crying for their mothers. I am more than a mile away but I can still hear them. The mother cows are too far away to be heard, but I know that they are as strident in their distress.

The impetus for both mother and child is a physiological one. The calves are hungry. The cows' udders hurt.

Having breastfed both my children, I can relate. I remember the tightness that graduated to an ache and then to outright pain. It was the only time in my life that I had sizeable breasts. I felt like a two-legged dairy cow with a girth to match her expanded bust line.

For several days, the noise will continue. No soothing lullaby this, more a cacophony of dissonant sounds. Where is my baby? I want my mommy.

But then the swollen, tender udders will shrink. The babies will learn to assuage their hunger with grain, hay, and water. But there is more to mother's milk than sustenance, and no other food will ever be as comforting.

Sometimes older animals give in to the urge for a forbidden suck long after they have been officially weaned. We tried nose rings to help them stop, but even that remedy wasn't foolproof. The nose rings make it difficult to get close to a teat—difficult, but not impossible. Few obstacles

36

are proof against determination. Often our only option was to sell the animal, which sometimes seemed a harsh penalty for immaturity.

It could be argued, I suppose, that a young calf won't get enough to eat if an older animal is stealing all the milk from its mother. Or, if you look at it another way, what kind of mother would a still-sucking heifer make? Too concerned about her own needs to look after another's.

I am also not sure whether cows recognize other cows in the herd as their own progeny. Certainly there are no family get-togethers as such, no gatherings of the clan to mark special occasions. When eventually we brought the cows home, they paid no special attention to the calves that had been taken from them several months earlier.

Cows are not people, of course. Bovine motherhood is purely biological, whereas human beings complicate things with emotional attachments. I have two children. I cannot imagine forgetting that I gave birth to either one of them. Different as night and day those two, their births impossible to forget.

When Lynne left home, I used to sit in her old room and listen to the silence. It was full of loud echoes. Glen attended university for two years to get his agriculture diploma, but he was home every weekend and all holidays. When he graduated, he returned to stay. So his room became a place I seldom ventured inside, too cautious of invading his territory. It was Joe and I who moved into rooms with no echoes at all. It seemed best after Joe's stroke to be in town closer to medical care. Best to let Glen and Susan on their own. Not easy, though.

I wander through the graveyard, the autumn sunshine

touching my skin with pleasant warmth. Here my grand-father's grave, beside it my grandmother's. Over there another set of grandparents. When we were young, a visit to this cemetery was part of our Father's Day ritual. After supper, we would drive my grandmother here to visit her husband's grave. And then we would spend time wander-ing, as I am doing now, before going home for coffee and cake at my grandmother's house.

"How many dead people are there in this cemetery?" my dad would ask. And when we said we didn't know, he came out with the punch line.

"All of them."

I think he kept that joke in his shirt pocket where it polished itself against the fabric and emerged shining and new again every year. Even when we were older and the joke no longer new, we still responded with laughter. It was a magic trick that, even when its secret was revealed, continued to amaze.

In the far reaches of the cemetery there are graves with headstones so weathered and worn that it is impossible to read the words engraved there. I do not know if anyone comes to visit these graves, or if those seeking family his-tory walk past them unknowing.

There are tiny headstones, Baby This and Baby That— human beings who spent such a short time here on earth they were never named. One family has three of these in a row. Imagine the heartbreak.

And in another row, the graves of four young children who died in a house fire from which only the mother and a fifth child escaped. Where was the dad? He worked for the railroad, I think. I have forgotten the story my grandmother told us, or at least I have forgotten that one detail.

I should be going; I am going to stop at the farm to see how the day went. I imagine they will be heading back out to the pastures after supper, checking to make sure that no calves were left behind and that no cows have broken fences in their attempts to follow their calves to the farmyard.

Mother cows have the advantage of experience; they know their way home. The calves, on the other hand, are lost.

I have returned to my mom and dad's graves, but instead of picking up the empty pails and going back to the car, I sit down on the grass and reach one arm out to trace the letters of my mom's name on the headstone with my fingers.

My mother died of pancreatic cancer. We could be thankful, I suppose, that the disease claimed her quickly although the idea of giving thanks for any of that experience seems laughable. My dad's death almost 20 years earlier was a different kind of sorrow, mixed as it was with the shock of the unforeseen. Going to town for repairs, Dad failed to notice an oncoming freight train as he crossed railway tracks he had crossed almost every day for thirty years.

"Now you are orphans," a neighbor said to me following my mom's funeral service.

"I guess so," I said and told my sisters about his comment. Adults cannot be orphans, we decided. Such an easy dismissal, I think now.

I used to dream of my mom often. Once I dreamed that

she was dying and, in the way that waking thoughts often intrude, I said to myself, "Why am I dreaming this? She's already dead."

Other times I dreamed that we were young again and Mom had left the family for another life somewhere. She went with another man, our dad said. She came back to visit and I angrily asked her why she left.

"I needed to," she said. "You don't know what a hard man your dad was to live with."

Another time I dreamed that I was picking my children up from school, a school that they never in real life attended. I was sitting in the hallway waiting for classes to end and there at the other end of the hall was my mother.

"What are you doing here?" I asked her.

"I want to see my grandchildren," she answered.

"But you went away years ago. Why do you want to see them now?"

I have never told anyone, not even Joe, about the dreams. We must learn to walk around the holes left in our lives when our parents die. But they are like shadows that trace the contours of our bodies with the movement of the sun and not always easy to avoid.

The sound of an approaching vehicle alerts me and I look up. Susan. I reach for the pails and move to greet her.

When I was young, my mother used to sing me a bedtime lullaby. Lullaby and goodnight, Mr. Sandman is calling. She would sing the song three times. Three times was her limit; she had other children to attend to and housework to finish.

When the song was over she would sit quietly for a minute or two before leaving my bedroom. I was seldom asleep, but I never opened my eyes. To this day I do not know whether she realized that I was faking sleep. I never told her and she never asked.

I would listen then for the sounds of her washing dishes, talking to Dad, feeding my sisters. Most of the time I was content to listen to her presence in the house and know that she was near. But sometimes I was upset that she had left me awake and alone. Shouldn't a mom know when you're pretending?

~ SUSAN ~

The cows got to stay in the pasture a while longer and after a few days, both young and old animals had quieted and seemed if not content, then at least resigned.

One morning the phone rang; a neighbour told us that they would be bringing their animals out of pasture and herding them down our road.

"Could someone stand in the driveway to prevent the animals from entering your yard?"

"That someone would be me," I said. "Do you know what time?"

"We'll stop at the house and let you know."

So two hours later there I was standing out at the end of our driveway, brandishing a long stick for waving around in the air, not for striking. Our own cattle knew the route so well that my presence would be unnecessary. They would go past the driveway without even glancing toward sthe house. But other cattle, unfamiliar with the terrain, might see an open driveway as an invitation.

Oftentimes just the fact that there is a human being standing there is good enough. The cattle see a stranger and veer away. Sometimes the person with the stick needs to wave her arms around and yell. Other times an animal will break from the string and get past her and then she has to run and head it off at the pass, so to speak.

The animals were being herded by farmers on horseback. We don't have horses; we use our truck and an all-terrain vehicle. But watching my neighbours ride past, legs in stirrups, horse hoofs clipping the ground in short staccato bursts, I could almost convince myself I was watching an old movie in 3D. Until, that is, I saw one of the riders pull a cell phone out of his jacket. A techy cowboy with one foot in the old world and the other in the new. I raised my hand in greeting as he rode past.


Elaine Benson, Joan's cousin, decided to sell the family herd after her husband's death, and selected the Saturday of the Thanksgiving weekend as the date for a disbursal sale. By scheduling the sale for then, she was able to avoid the additional costs of feeding the animals over the winter. Her husband had died of lung cancer earlier in the year and neighbours had helped her calve out the cows last spring and also kept an eye on them for her in pasture over the summer. Although the Bensons had four daughters, none of them lived here.

Glen and I attended not so much to purchase cattle as to see how the sale went and to see family members home for the weekend and the sale. Since they had just come off pasture, both the cows and their calves looked sleek and well-fed.

Neighbours and relatives had set up the panels for an outdoor sales ring. These same volunteers brought the animals into the ring and opened the gates to let them out and later lead them back to the pens after the bidding was over.

Mrs. Benson sat in a lawn chair surrounded by daughters, sons-in-law, and grandchildren. I thought she looked lost. Scuttlebutt was that her daughters were trying to persuade her to move off the farm and into town. My mother-in-law sat with her for a while.

I was in the same grade as the youngest Benson daughter Gail, although we had not been close friends. We had both been members of the local 4-H club and competed against each other over the years.

"That was my last 4-H heifer," I heard her say when a solid red Angus-cross cow came into the ring and I watched as her burly husband gave her a hug.

"Can we bid on this one?" I asked Glen.

"I thought you wanted us to go into purebreds, not add more crosses into the mix," he said.

"I do, but at least this is a red Angus, not black. And it was a 4-H heifer, so it will be quiet. It's been trained to lead."

"So you've done your good deed for the day," Glen said as we unloaded the cow and its calf later that afternoon.

"I guess," I said. "At least we know it's going to a good home."

"Says you."

I hosted the annual Thanksgiving meal for both sides of the family the day after the sale. Besides our parents, we invited Lynne and her family and my older brother Jon and his wife. Glen and I had decided that this would be a good opportunity to break the news about my pregnancy.

I was glad that the morning sickness seemed to have receded. Even so, everything looked and smelled not quite right and I had no appetite for any of it. I made the pumpkin pies from scratch and the yellow-brown filling reminded me of calf diarrhea. It was impossible to think of eating a piece of pie after that; it was difficult even to watch others put it in their mouths.

We had planned to make the announcement over dessert, but Dad beat us to the punch.

"You're eating too much of your own cooking, my girl," he told me. "Getting a little thick around the middle."

At that point, I hadn't gained any weight at all. In fact, I had lost a pound or two. And who wants to be told they're gaining weight? No one. But it was a perfect opening for my husband.

"She'll get thicker yet," Glen said. "She's in calf."

My brother Jonathan's two boys, Damian, 7, and Joel, 4, thought it was great that they would have a new cousin.

"Is it going to be a boy cousin or a girl cousin?" they wanted to know.

"We don't know yet," Glen said.

"You mean like the baby comes out of Auntie Susan's tummy and yells 'surprise'?" Joel asked.

"Sort of," I answered.

"Does Uncle Sam know?" Damian asked. My brother Sam lives in Vancouver.

"No, not yet, but we're going to phone him soon to tell him," I said.

The Triple As had other questions. Did we know what we were going to call the baby? Had we bought any clothes for the baby yet? Adam had some old toys he was willing to donate. Well, on second thought, maybe he was willing to lend them out if we promised to give them back.

"That's why you've been looking a little worn around the edges," Mom said as she gave me a hug.

Wonderful, I thought. I'm fat and frayed with more than six months still to go. Can life get any better than this?

My friend Carol only had three more months to go and a two-year-old to keep herself occupied in the meantime. We dropped in to visit Carol and her husband Bill one evening a week or so later so that we could tell them our news.

"I knew it!" Carol said. "No beer. No wine. I told Bill weeks ago that you were pregnant."

Carol didn't go back to work after her first child and, with the second one on the way, she had no plans to return anytime soon.

"Are you going to quit work?" she asked.

"Haven't even thought about it yet," I said. "But probably not."

Carol was big into early child development and she had recently attended a seminar on attachment.

"What's that?" I asked.

"Bonding with your child."

"But don't all parents bond with their child? Isn't it instinct, like a cow licking its calf?"

"You'd be surprised. We've gotten so into the 'things' we

45

want to give our kids that we've forgotten the importance of just being with them," Carol said. "When you have your baby, you'll have to come to our parent-child sessions."

Carol talks as if she's reading from a textbook. She didn't used to be that way until she had her first baby, or at least I never noticed it. Motherhood made her a student of all things maternal. A student and then a teacher. Whether people like me wanted to be taught or not.

What "things" did I want to give to my child? I'd never thought about it, although I suppose when the time came, I would be just as caught up in the sports teams and technological gadgets as anyone else.

"If we had a little boy, what would you want him to have?" I asked Glen that night after we had returned home.

"One of those made-to-scale John Deere tractor toys," he said.

In any community, there are the haves and the have-nots. Where I live the "haves" own green tractors. The "have nots" make do with red. I married up, although Dad would disagree. He has always preferred his red tractors. To hell with what the Joneses are buying.

Later I realized I had asked Glen what he would want to give a son and not what he would want to give a daughter. Why was that, I wondered. God forbid after all this time I was buying into the male descendent thing.

Carol's question about whether or not I would continue working after the baby was born also plagued me. I didn't know. I thought that economics would dictate the final answer. Although our crops had been good this year, so had almost everyone else's in the country. That meant that the price per bushel went down. Even with the best management practices possible and a nod from the heavens, the price still went down. How's a person supposed to get ahead that way? I knew few farmers' wives who could afford to stay home with their young children. Carol could count herself lucky.

But there was something else deeper down that bothered me. I wasn't sure that I wanted to quit work. It wasn't just about the pay cheque. It was about wanting the validation that work gave me. Was that a mark against me right from the start?

Mom told me not to worry about it.

"Take your time," she said.

Our harvested fields were full of both Canada and snow geese. I heard their calls throughout the day. It is impossible to deny the season when geese are flying overhead.

I am not a poet; my Grade Eleven English teacher told me I lacked the "soul of a poet," whatever that is. But whenever I hear geese in flight, I want to write poetry.

The lonely cries, the v-shaped formations, mating for life. There is more than one poem there. How the geese's departure coincides first with the colours of autumn and then with denuded trees and piles of browning leaves. And how their reappearance in the spring coincides with colour's return. Cycles and circles.

And if I wanted to inject humour, I could write about prairie pigeons with their propensity for pooping everywhere.

As the last of the leaves fell from the trees in our yard, I hung Halloween decorations from the bare branches. White ghosts shivered in the chill air. I carved a pumpkin.

I am no artist. The face on the finished product was askew and, in attempting to give the mouth some teeth, I had accidentally cut too far. There was a huge gap where a front tooth should have been, giving my jack-o-lantern a disreputable air. Jack was a down-on-his-luck pumpkin with no money for a dentist.

I wanted to be ready for the few Halloween kids we'd get. I think I inherited that interest in decorating from Mom. She divided the year into colours and decorated her house accordingly. My dad and brothers teased her, accusing her of going overboard, but I didn't agree with them. Mom decorated with colour, not with things, and the result was never cheesy. I'm not sure my efforts are as successful as hers, but I make an attempt.

"Next year we can take our kid out trick-or-treating," Glen said as he watched me fill the treat bags and took a chocolate bar for himself.

"You think so? She'll only be about six months old. She won't know what candy is."

"More for us then," he laughed. "So you think it is a girl?"

"No, I don't know whether it's a he or a she. The 'she' just came out."

Truth was, I was spending a lot of time pondering the he/she thing. I never knew which gender would pop out of my mouth.

Halloween's imminence signaled a change in the weather, which wasn't surprising. I don't remember too many years when October 31 was sunny and mild. It was the kind of weather that invited lazy afternoons under the covers and Glen and I took advantage of it one day. We had just barely begun the foreplay when I heard a knock at the kitchen door. I peered out the bedroom window, wondering why the dogs had not barked to warn us of company.

"It's my mom," I said and scrambled back into jeans and sweatshirt. It took long enough for me to get to the door that she had turned to go back to her vehicle.

"Mom," I called. "Sorry, I was upstairs and didn't hear you."

"I came for coffee," Mom said.

Partway through our first cup, Glen came into the kitchen, stretching as if he had just woken from a nap.

"Is there enough for me?" he asked. He stayed for one cup, then made his excuses and left.

"I came at a bad time, didn't I?" Mom asked.

"No, not at all," I said.

"I'm a married woman. You think your dad and I haven't had afternoon sex?"

The thought of Mom and Dad being caught out in an act of connubial bliss almost made me laugh. But then I thought she might be setting the scene for one of her stories. I knew just what to do to stop her.

"Gosh darn, Ma, you're hurting my ears," I said and covered them.

The "gosh darn" line was my younger brother Sam's; I'm not sure where he got it from. Our mother insisted that her children accept that parents were people, too. That they had the same anatomical parts as everyone else and that they used them in the same way. Bathroom noises were a part of being human and you wouldn't be here if your dad and I weren't sexually active. She drew parallels

49

between the mating rituals out in the pasture and those in the human world.

But when you're a teenager, the idea of your parents coupling—the images inspired by that idea—are unnerving. We preferred to think of our mother as the Virgin Mary, although we never stopped to consider what that might mean about our dad.

So Sam, the youngest and silliest of us, began using his line whenever she verged too near uncomfortable territory. It always worked; she would laugh.

"Your ears need toughening up," she would say.

It worked again today. Mom laughed and reached for her coffee. I knew she would not tell her story, but I think she was reliving it.

## ~ SANDRA ~

I hear a vehicle coming behind me and know without turning that it is our red Ford half-ton. I move over to the side of the gravel road, dusty prairie grass lightly flouring my shoes.

"Want to come for a ride?" Dave asks as he pulls up beside me. "I'm going up north to check the cattle."

I hesitate.

"You don't want to?" my husband asks.

"Yeah, sure," I say and walk over to the passenger side, stopping briefly to pat our dog Dingo who is cadging a ride in the truck box.

"You must have caught up on the baling," I say. It is

shortly after seven, more than two hours of sunlight still remaining in the day.

"Yep," he says. A man of few words, my husband. Over the almost twenty years of our marriage, our communication has become abbreviated, a shorthand at which each is now proficient. When Dave says "dog food" I know that he means "we are low on dog food, so pick some up the next time you go to town."

I watch the ditches and fields pass as we drive the four miles to the north pasture. Mid-July and the vivid colours of spring have lost their clarity. Mottled green leaves hang in a sun-drenched haze. The heat clings to the day with sticky fingers.

The freshly-cut hay in the fields smells like honey with a hint of mint. I breathe it in with pleasure.

"You were going for a walk?" Dave asks.

"Yep," I say, consciously echoing his earlier reply. I like to go for walks in the early evening. Not necessarily for the exercise, although that is an easy enough justification. More for the solitude. Thinking time, I call it. Although I don't spend much time thinking. I just walk, senses soaking in the sky and the ground and the space between. The silence is a comfort, rather than a void that needs filling.

"You didn't have to come with me," Dave says. "Sorry if I disturbed your walk."

"No problem. I would have said if I didn't want to come." To myself I admit this is what they used to call a little white lie, an untruth voiced in the pursuit of peace and good manners. I don't easily give up my alone time.

When we reach the approach to the pasture, I get out to open the gate and pull the posts out of the way, letting my husband drive through. Then I stretch the barbed wire back across the opening, hooking the loop over the end post to hold the gate in place.

I get back into the truck and we drive into the pasture. It is a bumpy ride over ground gouged by the passage of many hooves. I look through the back window to see the dog lose its balance and stumble. It is back on its feet in seconds, shoulders braced against the next shudder of the vehicle, eyes scanning the horizon for any sign of movement.

I'm not the only one who knows the sound of our half ton. The cattle recognize it, too. The pasture seems empty at first, but one by one, the cows start to come out of the bush where they had been seeking shade. The calves follow their lead.

The summer has been kind to the animals, I think. Their bellies are full and their coats shine. The calves have lost the frisky legginess of the newborn and are filling out.

We drive towards the centre of the open grazing area. Dave gets out. Dingo jumps out of the back, already at a run. He circles round the cows and calves, drawing them in ever closer to the truck. Dingo is an Australian cattle dog; herding cattle is in his genes. Soon Dave and I are surrounded by cows and their offspring.

"Help me count," he says.

I climb into the back of the half-ton to get a better view. We brought twenty-eight matching cow-calf pairs out to this pasture in May. Now we need to assure ourselves that none are missing. Perhaps there are some laggards still hiding in the shade. That would mean we would need to spend time searching. Less pleasant alternatives include a sick animal lying in some quiet corner or, worse, a dead one. There are hidden dangers in the pasture—unseen holes that can cause an animal to break a leg, noxious plants, even illegal snares left from winter trap lines. There are predators, too, to worry about, both the two and the four-legged kind. We once found a young heifer with its hind quarters savagely gouged. Nature is not kind. In that instance, the gun my husband wielded had been the kindness.

Counting is not the easy task it should have been. The cattle mill around us, seldom standing still. It requires concentration.

"I only get twenty-seven," Dave says.

"I got twenty-nine," I say.

We count again.

"Twenty-eight," we both say at the same time. All present and accounted for.

Dave begins to walk among the animals, checking that each cow has a calf at foot and looking for any signs of illness or injury. I return to the front seat and watch.

I like coming out to see the cattle in pasture and am always glad when in spring it is time to move them out of the corrals in the farmyard. It is good to see cows when I look out the living room window or when I walk out to the garden or am cutting grass. And when summer is high and bees are buzzing in the hay crops, the season is complete.

Life does not get any better than this, I think. A cow and its calf, endless days of green grass and summer sunshine, a herd bull for protection and fertilization when the time is right. I call it the summer of their contentment.

The bull comes sauntering out of the bush, a late arrival. Tough life, managing his harem. The shade is his right and privilege. But something more than curiosity has drawn him out now, I see. I watch as the bull comes up on a cow, sniffing her from behind.

Dave watches, too, irritation in his face.

"I think it's time we took the bull out," he says.

Bulls are always removed from the pasture before late summer to prevent late calves. But any cow not already in calf when the bull is removed will not get in calf that year. That means a year of feed and veterinary expenses with nothing going into the bank account to balance it out. If it happens more than two years in a row to the same cow, a decision has to be made about whether or not to keep her in the herd. It pays to be fertile.

There is another consideration as well. By mid to late summer, female calves are like precocious twelve-year-olds, capable of reproduction but in no way prepared for it. An early unplanned pregnancy could have lasting health consequences for the heifer. But robbing from the cradle means nothing to a bull, who just reads the signs and acts on them.

This male, for example, knows a female in heat when he smells one. And we can be thankful, I suppose, that the cow in question is a mature lady. A late calf would be an annoyance, nothing more. Certainly Dave will not intervene. You don't stand between a 2500-pound bull and his woman. Some battles are not worth fighting.

The female, however, did not appear completely compliant.

"Maggie, you vixen you," I say and Dave laughs.

"Typical female," he says. "Not tonight, dear. I have a headache."

"That's lame," I say. "I don't think cows get headaches."

"Maybe not, but if they get a stomach ache, it's four times worse than a human's."

I groan. "That's lamer yet," I say.

We watch the bedroom scene unfold before us.

Maggie is playing coy. When the bull approaches, she walks away. He follows. She moves again. Catch me if you can, she says. Done, he says.

With solid force, he launches himself on top of her, hind legs taking the brunt of his weight as he thrusts forward.

There is none of this up and down, in and out nonsense; one forceful penetration is all it takes. A violent shudder and it is over.

The bull dismounts and the cow walks away, her private parts gaping. Bovine erotica, I think, and shiver.

I feel Dave's eyes on me. I turn and catch the question in them.

"Do you want to?" he asks.

"Yes," I say, surprising myself. No coyness here.

"Where? Here?" he asks.

The plastic seat sticks to my legs. "No," I say and point to a stand of poplar trees, their branches a canopy over the grass below. "It will be cooler there."

"We don't have a blanket," he says.

"That never stopped us before."

"True. Remember the time in the garden?"

"Yes," I say. "That was a long time ago."

It had been in our pre-children days, later in the season when the corn was ready for picking. Dave came out to the garden where I was working and the idea occurred to both of us at the same time.

"Remember how hot it was?" I ask now. The air between the tall rows of corn had been sauna-like. It took our breath away. I can remember how heavy the air had felt and him on top of me. From beneath him I had looked up to see thin strips of blue sky between the corn stalks. Slivers of sunlight penetrated my body.

We had had an argument the night before, I remember, and the still unresolved dispute had given an edge to the act of love-making. There had been as much violence as tenderness in the act. Yet it had put to sleep the remnants of our anger.

The poplar trees today are a somewhat cooler alternative. We use our clothing as a blanket. An unsatisfactory arrangement. In our haste, we didn't think of zippers that dig into flesh or the discomfort of cowboy denim hardened by grime. Nor are there enough clothes to adequately cover the ground beneath us. Blades of grass sharpened by weeks without rain cut into bare skin.

I look at my husband's body, the lines where tan meets skin that never sees the sun. I kiss that line below his neck. So familiar, I could find it in the dark. He tastes of clover and salt.

Our bodies fit together with the ease of a learned habit. We have danced this dance so many times before, I think, although the metaphor is inappropriate. Dave does not dance. Except here between my legs. Here his movements are sure, knowing when to slow the pace, when to speed it up, when to lead and when to follow.

The edges are gone, I think. They've been washed away

by time and children, like land eroded by wind and water. Everything is smooth; we slide easily towards orgasm.

A blast of '80s music brings our slide to an abrupt stop. Dave and I freeze as if stillness could camouflage flesh against the colours surrounding it. A blue sedan hurtles past in a cloud of dust.

"Talk about coitus interruptus," I say, wanting to lighten the moment but needing to ask the question. "Did you recognize the car?"

"No," he says.

That's good, I think. It could have been one of our children. Never mind poor Sam's ears; he might have been blinded for life.

Dave begins to dress, pulling his jeans and shirt out from under me and shaking them free of grit before putting them back on. Before I have even stood up, he is heading back towards the truck.

Cows, calves, and bull—not a voyeur among them— have returned to the shade. Dingo is back in the truck box waiting for the ride home. Dusk draws in, blurring the edges of the day.

I dress more slowly, mindful that the car could return, yet unable to summon speed or energy. I feel as if I had watched an action movie that, despite its promise, fizzled badly at the end. Anti-climax is exactly the right word for it, I think, and reach for my underwear.

When I get to the truck, Dave is already inside, hands gripping the wheel.

"Time to go," he says.

"Yep," I say.

# FIVE

Susan. *That is my name. Born Susan Angela Connor. Now Susan Davidson, married to Glen Davidson, son of Joseph Davidson. Nobody calls him Joseph though. He is Joe to everyone. Except for Glen and his sister. They call him Dad. Ha. Laugh until you cry.*

*Funny thing. It's my dad who's named David. My brothers are the real David's sons.*

*My initials, now that I'm married, are SAD. The strange things you think of when you're trying to focus on other things. No sex, no alcohol, no drugs. So SAD. Perhaps I should have kept my birth surname. Then I could be a sad SAC. That's going from bad to worse.*

*Things that come in fives: Five fingers on your hands. Five toes on your feet. Things we want our baby to have. Please let it come with the right number of fingers and toes. And with all five of its senses: sight, hearing, smell, touch, and taste. Five vowels in the alphabet: a, e, i, o, u. Ignoring "y." Five cents in a nickel. The five Ws—who, what, when, where, why. Five days in a school or work week. High five. Fifth wheel. Five gold rings. The Dionne quintuplets. Cancel that. Think positive.*

*Five is halfway to ten.*

"He left his wife," Lynne told me when we met for coffee one Friday afternoon in early November. I had come in for a doctor's appointment. "I don't know what to do."

"Do you need to do anything?" I asked.

"Well, I feel guilty," she said. "Maybe he left her because of me."

I wanted to hit her over the head with the coffee urn. A spoon in the eye might have worked. But the coffee urn would have made a bigger splash and drowning her in liquid caffeine seemed appropriate. Call it a wakeup call.

She felt guilty because her married lover left his wife, but I hadn't yet heard her say that she felt any guilt for having an affair herself.

I asked her once this fall what was wrong with her marriage.

"Nothing," she said. "Sometimes it's not about what's wrong with what you have. It's about what might be right with what you don't," she said.

I took a few moments to follow that through. It was convoluted, although it did make a certain amount of sense in a "grass is greener on the other side of the fence" kind of way. It's not, of course, but the possibility that it might be is enticing.

"Has he asked you to come with him?" I asked.

"No," she said. "He hasn't."

"Would you go with him if he did?"

"I don't know."

Neither did I.

My doctor said we could know the baby's gender if we wanted. Glen and I both said no. Bill and Carol knew she was having a girl this time round, but Glen and I were looking forward to the surprise at the end of the pregnancy. Although, how much of a surprise could it be? There were only two options—a boy or a girl. Twins would be a surprise all right, but we already knew that I wasn't having twins. Besides I knew a woman who badly wanted a girl because she already had a son and didn't plan a third pregnancy. When the tests indicated another boy, she went into a funk that lasted the next five months. Then it turned out that there had been a clerical error; it was a girl after all. A happy ending, but I just remember all those months of sadness. Better not to know.

We had selected an upstairs bedroom as the new baby's room and I wanted to paint it yellow, the colour of sunshine. If my baby is a girl, I will paint the trim white. Blue if it is a boy.

Mom offered to help me paint. She thought we should start right away.

"We can wait a while, can't we? It's only November," I said.

"Yes, but after November comes December and with Christmas and everything, there will be no time then. And as you get further and further along, you won't feel much like doing it. Believe me, I know."

So I bought the paint and she and I spent the greater part of a week getting the job done. It took us longer than we had thought it would because the walls were covered with several layers of wallpaper, which I wanted to remove before painting.

Peeling off the wallpaper was like going back in time, decade by decade and pattern by pattern. A green with gold flecks that I thought hideous. A floral pattern in greens and pinks. A geometric maze of blues and purples. Splashing on the paint was easy after that.

"Pregnancy is divided into three parts," Mom told me as we rolled the paint onto the walls. "The first three months are the blah months. You may have morning sickness. Food doesn't taste quite right. The second trimester is the golden time. You begin to show. Life is wonderful. And then the last three months are the heavy months when you are carrying the weight of the world in your belly and you cannot wait for it to be all over."

The finished walls were brighter than I had imagined when I looked at the colour in the store, but not over-whelmingly so. It would do.

It was during that week of painting that one of our herd bulls began to limp.

"I think we're going to need to buy a new bull," Glen said at supper. A bull with an injured leg is just as bad as a bull with a low semen count. We started thumbing through the sale catalogues as they arrived in the mail and browsing online, searching for a suitable replacement.

There are many things to consider when selecting a new bull, everything from scrotal circumference (size really does matter) to historical data on the animal's birth, weaning, and yearling weights.

One of my jobs at the vet clinic is to assist the vet with breeding evaluations. I hold the animal while my boss handles the tape measure. Or vice versa. Whichever works best. It's a good gag line at parties. How was work today? I measured a bull's balls.

Glen and I took a drive to look at some bulls included in a purebred sale early in December. One of them, a solid black two-year-old, took an interest in me and followed me all the time we were in the bullpen.

"Just wave him away," the owner said. "He won't hurt you, but he can be a pest."

If the black pest thought he was going to influence our choice by being extra friendly, like a youngster in an orphanage scoping out prospective parents, it was doomed to disappointment. We did not want a black bull.

But we disagreed over which animal we might want. I had my eye on a smaller full red bull; Glen preferred the looks of a rangier animal with red and white markings.

"Yours would be a good heifer bull," he said. "But we want a herd bull."

He was right.

# SIX

*Things that come in sixes: Six packs. Sides on a cube. Legs on an insect. Six geese a-laying. Six feet under. There have to be more, but my mind has gone blank. Focus, Susan, focus. I can't. I am going into panic mode.*

*Why did I want this in the first place? Blame sex. Sex got me into this. I swear the first male appendage I see, I'm going to stick it somewhere and it won't be anywhere that would make a baby.*

*Glen is back from his shopping expedition. His hair looks shorter.*

*"Did you get a fucking hair cut?" I ask.*

*"I've never heard her swear in public before," Glen says to the nurse.*

*"Time and a place for everything," the nurse says as she flicks a clump of hair from the collar of his blue plaid work shirt.*

*Six is half a dozen; maybe I can think of things that come that way. A half dozen eggs. A half dozen donuts. A half dozen roses. Six of one and a half dozen of the other. Sixth sense. At sixes and sevens.*

*Why is six afraid of seven? Because seven eight nine.*


We went to the bull sale, but didn't get the animal we wanted. It went for more money than we could afford.

My family used to participate in auction sales, but not so much these days. We raised purebred animals and sold them as breeding stock. I remember days spent hauling the bulls or heifers to the sale site, usually in the winter when it was cold and the trip was often on icy roads.

We would unload our animals into a big barn where they would be placed in a specially-assigned pen. For the next day, we would feed and groom them. Someone always stayed near the pen in case a potential buyer had any questions about the animal. Questions about birth weight and lineage. Genetics are important. Disposition is, too. Since my head was full of those details, I was often the family member given this job. But we always had a paper folder on hand in case we needed to refresh our memories on a certain point.

The first animals to go into the ring were determined by the sale's organizers to be the best animals of the sale and were almost always guaranteed the highest prices of the day. One of us would accompany our animal into the sales ring. We would be lined up in order of sale and moved forward until it was our turn. Then we would lead our animal into the ring and a door would slide shut behind us to prevent the animal from escaping. The idea was to lead the animal around the ring several times, then position it in the centre of the ring so that buyers could get a good look at what was on offer.

I did not enjoy my time in the sales ring. It's one thing to lead an animal around in a show ring where there is plenty of space to manoeuvre. It is another to stand in a cramped space with bid takers yelling and the auctioneer barking into a microphone. Even the most docile of animals found it stressful.

And yet it was important that they remained passive in the face of this barrage of light and sound. If an animal got away from its handler and acted out, which often happened and wasn't surprising when it did, buyers would hesitate to bid. No one wanted to buy an animal that was difficult to handle, one that could prove dangerous on the farm. Totally understandable, but unfair to the animal, I always thought.

I preferred it when buyers would come to the farm and see our animals in their natural setting. Less stress on everyone, animal and human alike.

When the sale was over, the winning bidders would line up to pay for their purchases and the (former) owners would head back to the barn to greet the buyers when they returned and offer them a drink to celebrate the transaction. Now that the work was over, there was time to socialize. And my brothers and I would almost always slip into the pen to say goodbye to the animal, which would soon be loaded up and trucked to its new home.

In the end Glen and I bought a two-year-old bull privately from a breeder who lived a couple of hours away. It was an excuse for another Sunday afternoon drive. This was a full red bull to suit my preference, but with a build that Glen preferred. Best yet, the price was right.

By that time, we had moved all the cows home to the yard. We keep the cows out in pasture as long as we can. Even after the green grass is gone, we keep them there, hauling bales of hay out every morning. But once there is snow on the ground, and once we get within a month or so of calving season, we move them home where we can keep a closer eye on them.

The first snow arrived in mid-December, later than usual, although none of us were complaining. Climate change seems to be showing itself lately in extreme weather but the past few months had been storm-free.

That morning of the first snow, I followed Glen out to the barn and stopped to pick up a handful of snow just to see what it felt like. It was the perfect consistency for snowballs, wet enough to make the flakes cling together. I scooped up more snow and made one in my hands.

"Glen!" I called.

When he turned around, I pasted him in the chest. Within seconds we were in the middle of an all-out snowball fight, moving closer to each other so that our aims would be truer. I started the fight, but I knew I would not win it. When I took a step backwards, my feet slipped and I fell heavily.

Winded, I lay there looking up at a sodden grey sky, arms splayed out, fingers clutching at snow.

Glen came running.

"Are you all right? The baby?" he asked.

I lifted my right arm and aimed another snowball at him.

"You little ..." he said and pinned me to the ground with his arms. We were both laughing.

"Careful, now," I said. "I'm the mother of your unborn child, don't forget."

Our two dogs were jumping around us, eager to join the play. Glen helped me up and we continued our walk to the barn.

Later that night I found an advertisement in an online catalogue for a plastic snowball maker. It resembled a pair of tongs with circular scoops at each end. When you pressed the tongs together, the snow inside the scoops formed into a perfectly round snowball. Plus, the advertisement promised, your mitts won't get wet or your hands cold. It seemed silly to me. Who cares whether the balls are perfectly round? I tried to imagine our morning snowball fight, each of us using our purchased snowball maker, and Glen wondered why I was laughing out loud. He just shook his head when I showed him.

"A fool and his money," he said. Sometimes my husband sounds just like his dad.

"The more I learn about people, the more I like my cows," I said.

"Your grandfather?"

"No, me."

I might have lied, though. Maybe I did hear it first from Grandpa.

I suddenly realized what I wanted for my child. I wanted my child to know the seasons. I wanted to show him how to make snow angels and snowmen. I wanted him to throw snowballs and get his mitts wet. I wanted him to know what that felt like.

He or she, the baby was becoming more real to me.

"You are so lucky," I told my cow Evelyn.

She really is my cow. She was my last 4-H heifer and I moved her from Mom and Dad's farm after Glen and I got married. She's about eight years old now, and this would be her seventh calf.

Evelyn was lucky because she didn't need to buy maternity clothes. She was heavily in calf, but the brown hide that kept her covered all summer was still doing the job now. It was shaggier of course—nature's way of keeping her warm through the winter.

"And you don't have to buy baby stuff, either," I said as I scratched her. Whereas I had a long list of "need to buys" beside the grocery list on the refrigerator door.

- Crib and/or cradle
- Sheets and towels and baby facecloths
- Receiving blankets
- Diapers and a diaper bag
- Car seat
- Baby bouncer
- Sleepers
- Onesies (I had to ask about these, although I recognized what they were as soon as I was told.)
- Change table
- High chair
- Baby bathtub
- Soothers
- Rattles
- Breast pump

My friend Diane offered me her breast pump, but I said

no, thank you. I planned to buy my own, and I didn't think I'd ever offer it to anyone else.

And I hadn't made up my mind about diapers. Carol was pushing me to go green and invest in cloth diapers, but I wasn't sure how I could add the extra laundry to my workload without giving up sleep. I like my sleep.

No one asked what I wanted for Christmas; instead they asked "What do you need for the baby?"

I registered with "Babies R Us" to make their shopping easier.

"Your mom has something to tell you," Dad said, looking at everyone around the table before dipping his spoon in pudding and sauce. It was Christmas Eve.

Mom looked at him.

"Your dad *and* I have something to tell you," she said.

"Well, what is it?" my brother Jonathan asked. "Don't keep us waiting now that you have our attention."

"I am moving to the city after the New Year," she said.

"You're what?" I asked.

"I've enrolled at university and I'm going to stay with my friend Donna in her apartment."

Donna was a long-time friend, dating back to grade school. She had married young, divorced less than five years after the wedding, and never remarried. Mom occasionally spent a weekend in the city with her and every once in a (very long) while, Donna would arrive at the farm for an overnight visit. Dad always took himself off for the evening when Donna was there. It wasn't that he didn't like Donna; they just had different ideas about a lot of things.

"University? What are you taking?"

"Women's Studies," she said.

"She's trying to figure out what makes them tick," Dad interjected. "Then she's going to come home and tell me."

"And how do you feel about this, Dad?" This from Jonathan.

"Your mom's gotta do what your mom's gotta do," Dad said.

"But are you all right with it? Are you happy that she's doing this?"

"Your mom's gotta do what your mom's gotta do," Dad said again and that was the end of that.

Recent events became suddenly clearer.

"That's why you wanted to paint the baby's room in November," I said. "Because you knew you would be gone after Christmas."

"Guilty as charged," Mom said. "Although I didn't know for sure."

"But why keep it a secret?"

"I didn't find out I was accepted until just a week or so ago. Why get everyone all in a tizzy if it wasn't going to happen anyway?"

"But you never said anything. We never knew you wanted to go back to school."

"Your dad knew," she said.


"I can't believe she's doing this," I said to Glen on the drive home.

"I can," he said. "Your mom always follows her own piper."

"But she never said anything. She should have told us. And she won't be here when our baby comes."

"Well, she might, you know. Her exams could be done by mid-April."

"If she comes back after exams."

"You think she won't?"

"I don't know. She was pretty vague about it all. What if this is the start of a new life for her that dad and the farm aren't a part of?"

"She didn't say that."

"She didn't say much of anything and all Dad did was accept her decision as if he has no say in the matter."

"He probably doesn't." He laughed. "You could be proud of her, you know. She's doing something brave, I think."

If Mom and I have a disagreement, Glen always seems to take her side. It irritates the hell out of me.

"But she's not going to be here when I need her. I imagined her being with me when the baby came, living with us for a week or so. Being there when I called with questions. I don't know how to be a mother."

"Is that what it's about then? You're upset because your mom isn't fitting her life to your schedule? Maybe it's a pregnant thing, the way you're acting," he said.

Now I was just angry.

"Why does it come down to that? Why is everything with women always a hormone thing? Don't we have the right to feelings just because we feel them? Why do they have to be linked to our bodies?"

We were silent the rest of the way home. We brought in the presents we had received and the roaster of cabbage rolls I had taken as my contribution to the Christmas meal. Once the cabbage rolls were put away, I turned on the Christmas tree lights in the living room.

"Coming to bed?" Glen asked.

"In a bit," I said. "I think I'm going to sit for a while."

"We could have a Christmas drink," he said.

I rubbed the bump that defined me these days.

"I wish," I said.

"I could keep you company."

"I'd kinda like to be alone for a while," I said.

"Suit yourself."

I could tell he was hurt by the way he turned and walked up the stairs to the bedroom. I sat there in the almost darkness, feeling sorry for myself.

When I did climb into bed a half hour later, I curved my body around Glen's, resting my hand on his hip.

"I'm sorry," I said. "I feel like a spoiled little kid."

"No problem," he mumbled.

"Merry Christmas, Glen."

Glen turned to face me. He placed his hands on the swell of my tummy.

"Merry Christmas," he said.

In the morning, we followed the Christmas ritual we had begun after our marriage. We went out to do the morning chores together. We took our time and gave the cows, bulls, and weaned calves a little extra grain and hay. It was Christmas, after all.

# SEVEN

*Things that come in sevens. The days of the week. The Seven Dwarves. Seven years of bad luck if you break a mirror. Seven wives for seven brothers. Lucky seven. Seven Wonders of the World. Seven deadly sins. Canada's Group of Seven. Seven swans a-swimming.*

*The young woman in the next bed has been in labour for eighteen hours. Her husband brought her in last night and has remained by her side.*

*When the nurse asks her how she is doing, she says, "Great" and seems to mean it.*

*"The pain is not too bad?" the nurse asks.*

*"I can handle the pain. And my husband is here beside me in this wonderful journey that God is taking us on."*

*"I want to puke," I say and Glen brings over the puke bowl.*

*"No, I said I want to puke, not I have to puke. I want to puke. I hate them."*

*Glen grins.*

*"Me too," he says. "Want me to put a hit out on them?"*

*"Seems extreme," I say. "Maybe just put a curse on them. May they feel my pain."*


We went to Mom and Dad's for supper the night before Mom left for Winnipeg. The meal had an awkward Last Supper feel to it.

"What exactly are you going to learn in these Women's Studies of yours?" Jon asked.

"A lot of history, I think," Mom said. "Religious and cultural practices around the world."

"Are there Men's Studies?" Jonathan's seven-year-old wanted to know.

"No, I don't think there are."

"Why not?"

"That's a good question, Damian. I don't know why not. Maybe my Women's Studies will help me find out."

"Dad, you'll have to come over for supper lots," I said. "Or I can bring you casseroles and things."

"I can cook, you know," Dad said. "Although I appreciate the offer and I shall probably take you up on it from time to time. I'll probably be sponging off Jon and Andrea a lot, too."

"You look thrilled, Andrea," Glen joked.

Andrea threw her napkin at him.

"Dad is welcome at our house anytime and he knows it," she said.

Dad did know it. We all knew it. Andrea is one of those

translucent people who blends into our family without standing out. She has done so ever since Jon first brought her home to meet us. Without calling attention to herself, she became part of the family.

I have often envied that ability of hers. And it's not just here at family gatherings. The same thing applies wherever she is—at home, at school, at community events. It's as if she can expand or compress herself to fit available space, rounding out her edges or even forming a right angle if that is what is needed. She is part of the whole, rather than an add-on. I don't know how she does it.

"We phoned Sam today," Mom said.

My youngest brother usually makes it home once a year, but not often at Christmas. He had called Christmas Eve when we were all together and had talked to each of us in turn.

"What did he have to say?" Jon asked.

Dad laughed.

"He said, 'You go, Mom.'"

"I'm not going away forever, you know," Mom said. "I'll be home on weekends. Well, maybe not every weekend depending on the roads and weather and how much homework I have. But most weekends probably. And we have phone and Internet. You'll be hearing from me often.

"I want to thank you all for going along with me on this. I know it was a shock and perhaps your dad and I should have included you in our discussions about it. I worried that you might think it's a midlife crisis of some kind and you could be right. But maybe it's just a midlife change of direction. I am excited and scared about it. It has been a long time since I was a student. I need your support and I'm hoping I have it."

"Mom gave a speech," Jon said.

Everyone laughed. Speeches were not usually Mom's thing. But I wasn't sure what Mom's thing was anymore.

It was strange, not having her around. We could still talk on the phone and we texted each other. Mom even joined Facebook and invited me to be her friend. I hesitated before replying because I had never thought of my mother as a friend. She's my mother. But I didn't want to hurt her feelings and so I accepted her offer. She didn't seem to be on there much, which must have meant that she had other things to do.

But it was weird to not be able to go home and find her there. Dad didn't fill the house the way she did.

When he started phoning every evening, I knew he was lonely, but he wouldn't say so.

We sold the first load of steers early in the new year, wanting to be rid of their daily feeding before the cows started calving. It would just be too much work.

I got up with Glen early in the morning before the cattle truck arrived to take our steers to a feed lot in Alberta. I brewed a pot of strong coffee and poured it into a thermos to take to the driver. We loaded forty-five 900-pound animals into the back of the semi and I cried as the truck drove out of the yard.

I used to cry when I said goodbye to my 4-H steer every year. I loved showing heifers because I could bring them home again. But a steer had to be sold and butchered;

its carcass evaluation was one of the ways in which club members were graded on their year's project.

I'm a farmer's wife and a farmer's daughter. I'm not about to barricade the road so that the semi cannot get through. It's OK to kill to eat, not OK for anything else. They're not my words. An actor repeated them in a murder mystery on television the other night and they stuck in my head.

Still, I was sad when the steers left our yard. I was glad, however, to have fewer chores to do every day. Pretty soon we would be living the erratic hours of an obstetrician, finding brief hours of sleep between births.

That same day a Colorado low blew in, dumping fifteen centimetres of new snow and piling it in banks with eighty kilometre per hour wind gusts.

"Snow day!" I said, although in truth the weather made no difference to our plans. It was not a regularly scheduled work day for me at the clinic and we didn't need to go anywhere. Good for us that we had loaded the animals that morning before the weather turned; more luck than management, of course. I hoped that the semi driver wouldn't have too much trouble on the roads; I thought he would have few troubles since this was a Colorado low, and not an Alberta clipper. He would drive out of it fairly quickly.

Glen took advantage of the storm to catch an afternoon nap. Although I was tempted to join him, I succumbed instead to the lure of the attic. There was a trunk I had had my eye on for some time.

When I lifted the lid, however, I was disappointed. The trunk contained nothing but farm papers. Nevertheless, I started sifting through them. I wrapped myself up in an old afghan crocheted in shades of orange, brown, and green and sat down beside the trunk, listening to the wind howl around the corners of the house.

Here was the farm expense book for 1986 entered in Joan's tiny precise handwriting. She had written down each item, then ticked it back in red ink at the end of the year to ensure she had matching receipts for each entry. The receipts themselves were separated into categories— machinery expenses, fuel, vet bills, and the like—and stapled together in chronological order. At the end of the year, she totaled each category on an adding machine and stapled the paper to the appropriate page. Such diligence.

I am the bookkeeper nowadays and I cannot imagine that kind of paperwork. I enter each item into our accounting program and let the computer do all the arithmetic. It isn't perfect and sometimes there are mistakes, but those mistakes are always mine, not the computer's. I have miscoded something, for example, or forgotten to separate out the GST paid out on a purchase.

In 1986 there would have been no GST. When that was introduced in 1991, Joan must have had to manually deduct the tax from each bill and keep a separate total of tax paid for reporting purposes. No wonder people swore when the new tax was mentioned.

Their gross income in 1986 was $45,000. Glen's grandfather would have been alive at the time and I think he still had a share of the farm, so the income and expenses would have been split.

In 1986 their cattle sold for about $650 an animal, more for steers and heavier animals. I don't know if they considered 1986 a good year or a bad year. I do know that in recent years we have seen similar prices. Not much change in more than twenty-five years.

But there were lots of changes on the expense side of the ledger. Everything from fuel to taxes costs significantly more than it did in 1986.

If I owned a business that manufactured trunks, for example, I would charge enough for each trunk to cover the cost of the materials it was made of, the wages of the staff person making it, taxes and utilities for the building it was made in. If those costs went up, I could increase the price of the trunk to offset that increase. If I charged too little, my expenses would exceed my income and I would go bankrupt. If I charged too much, my sales would decline, my expenses would exceed my income, and I would go bankrupt. Tricky decisions, but there would be room for maneuvering, I think. And it would be my call.

It doesn't work that way for farmers. The weather is the predominant factor in the quality and quantity of our product and we have no control over the price of the product we do have for sale. Those prices fluctuate from week to week and are influenced by everything from politics to the price of rice in China.

I was tired of thinking about finances and turned to an old bookcase along the far wall. Tucked inside a hardcover copy of fiction by Nellie McClung I found a folded piece of onionskin paper. Inside the fold a crocus, so dry I did not dare touch it. A razor thin memory of a long ago spring. The book, printed in 1912, was a collection of short stories entitled *The Black Creek Stopping House*. There was no name inscribed on the flyleaf. I did not know who might have placed the crocus there for safekeeping. But there were words written in tiny, cramped script on the paper.

"If we had left it rooted in the prairie soil and let it drink in sunlight till springtime's end, would the lines of this love story have rhymed more perfectly?"

A sad memory then, whoever the crocus petals belonged to.

The storm became a blizzard that lasted into the next day and left snowbanks across our driveway. If there was ever a time and place for a blizzard, it was January in Manitoba. But the weatherman predicted much milder weather once this system passed through.

When the snow finally stopped, Glen and I went out to bed down the cows, laying fresh straw so that they could snuggle into it and keep warm.

Our heifers started calving around the middle of the month and although it was getting harder to find snowsuits that would go around my baby bulge, I waddled out daily after work and on weekends to see the young calves and to check for imminent births. I often took the midnight check, leaving the three a.m. walkabout to Glen. Other years, we had taken turns. But this year my swollen belly gave me a pass.

Except for the night Genie had her calf; Glen needed me that night.

The newborn calf gasped for air. Glen stuck a straw down one of its nostrils, trying to clear the airway, and then leaned over to blow directly into the animal's nose. But it was not enough. The calf shuddered and went still.

"I'm sorry, Genie," I said to the cow. Genie paid no

attention. Head down towards her infant calf, she fiercely licked off the detritus of birth as if she could bring back life as she had given it.

An hour earlier Glen had come to the house.

"Wake up," he said, throwing the bedroom light switch and jerking me out of sleep. "I need your help."

The unusual urgency in his voice made me dress quickly. The wind wrapped itself around me as I followed Glen down the packed snow trail. As predicted, the weather had turned after our January blizzard and temperatures were extremely mild for this time of year, but at two o'clock in the morning, the wind was raw.

In the shed two-year-old Genie stood, straining with the effort of giving birth to her first calf.

"One of its feet is bent back," Glen said. "Hold her tail, will you?"

I stood beside the cow, speaking softly and holding its tail so that my husband could work without obstruction. Glen pushed the calf back into the uterus, found the bent foreleg, and gently eased it into proper position. Then he attached chains to the calf's front legs and used traction to one leg at a time, walking the shoulders through the cow's pelvis and working in concert with the animal's contractions.

"It will be all right, Genie. Take it easy, girl."

But it was not all right. Although Glen was able to pull the calf, we could tell immediately that its future was precarious.

Perhaps if we had called the vet, a Caesarian could have been performed. Perhaps if Glen had gone out to check the cows earlier or had come back to the house to get me sooner. But what ifs are pointless. Some things just are.

"Let's see if Genie will take one of the twins," Glen said.

Three days earlier, another cow in the herd had given birth to twins. Twins are not uncommon; we often have several sets each year. But they are extra work because many times the mother cow won't have enough milk to feed two calves.

This particular cow did not. We had to supplement her milk, feeding the twins manually with a giant nipple attached by tubing to a plastic bag of formula. If a cow had extra milk, I froze it for future use. The real thing was better for calves, but I didn't always have any in the freezer.

"It's worth a try," I said.

Genie's udder was already filling, a physiological response to the act of giving birth. The cow continued licking her calf, alternately nudging it with her nose. Wake up, baby. The act of licking bonded mother to child. Genie had already learned the scent of her newborn; taking another calf in its place would now be more difficult.

I stayed with Genie until Glen came back with the larger of the twins, a red and white bull calf which seemed all legs. Its twin was a heifer calf, smaller and almost certainly sterile. Somehow that's the way it seemed to work. Twins of the same gender might or might not be fertile, but the female in a set of boy-girl twins faced a greater chance of never being able to reproduce.

By picking the larger and stronger of the two, Glen was giving the smaller calf a better chance with the natural mother. And the bull calf would be better able to handle any reluctance on Genie's part to cooperate.

The calf was willing and eager to sample Genie's teats. But Genie was having none of it. She stiffened as she felt the mouth reach for her, and then kicked out at the calf. Time and again we tried. Each time we failed.

They say that losing a child is like giving birth to the same child a second time, but without the release from pain that a successful delivery provides. I do not know if they are right. I do not want to know. There is pain in the thought of it.

"It's not going to work," I told Glen.

"Let's try something else," he said.

After tying the bull calf to a panel outside the pen, we dragged the corpse into a far corner.

"Want to hazard a guess at its weight?" I asked.

"A good hundred pounds, maybe more," he said. Poor Genie. No wonder there had been trouble. We had bred her to our heifer bull, a smaller animal that should sire smaller calves. Something had gone wrong somewhere.

He pulled a knife out of his overalls pocket and, while he began his work on the calf, I returned to the birthing pen, but did not enter it. Genie was increasingly agitated. As quiet a cow as she normally was, to approach her now might be dangerous. I positioned myself between mother and child. "Don't look," I said to the cow. "You don't want to know."

Once Glen had finished skinning the calf, he carried the hide over to the pen. He untied the twin and, as quickly as possible, flipped the calf over and rolled it in the slimy afterbirth still coating the floor. With any luck, the scent would fool Genie into accepting a replacement.

Then, as I held the twin steady, he carefully draped the hide over its back.

"Cross your fingers," he said.

He led the calf once more to Genie. At first Genie stiffened, but then nosed forward to sniff the hide. Glen held the calf still and we waited in silence for Genie to recognize and accept the scent. When Glen edged the calf towards the waiting teats, the calf grabbed hold and began to suck.

I should be relieved, I thought. It was a happy ending; the young heifer had a calf to feed, the older cow's burden was halved, the twins each had enough to eat. But instead I was angry. I wanted to yell at Genie. I wanted to hit her.

We tricked you, you stupid cow. This is not your baby.

They call it imprinting, don't they, the bonding between parent and child at first sight and touch? If I touched my baby and transferred that knowledge into some inner part of me, how could I possibly be fooled this way?

Once the calf had had its fill, it lay down on the straw beside its adopted mother. I brought over an armful of hay and Glen carried a pail of water into the pen. We stood and watched for several more minutes.

"I know it often works but I don't like doing it," Glen said. "It feels like cheating somehow."

"I know what you mean," I said.

We turned to leave the shed and headed back through the corrals to the house. I led the way and saw the cow first.

"We're not finished yet," I called. An eight-year-old cow, a veteran of the delivery room, was in the final stages of labour. There was no time to bring the cow into the shelter of the barn; birth was imminent.

We stood and watched Agnes heave and push, ready to lend a hand if problems became apparent. But this cow had no need of our services. Indeed she ignored our presence as if it were irrelevant.

With one last push, the slippery body exited the birth canal and slid onto the ground. Now Glen and I began our ritual. We wiped the calf as dry as we could and lifted it onto a sled built for this purpose. As we pulled the new calf, a spry, alert baby with legs already kicking, the mother cow followed us into the barn.

Once inside the pen, Agnes began to assiduously clean the calf with the rough edge of her tongue, scraping the new hide till it warmed from the abrasive treatment.

She looked at us as if to say, What're you two still doing here?

"Come on," Glen said. "Let's go get some sleep."

I gave one last look at the far corner where Genie and her adopted son rested, the hide still covering the three-day-old body.

"Everything is fine," Glen said, coming up behind me. "No worries."

"What am I, an open book?" I asked.

"Sus, I can read you from across the barn," my husband said.

For a long time, I wanted to be a veterinarian and look after animals—big ones, small ones, it didn't matter. But then I realized that there would be animals I couldn't make well. Even worse, there would be animals that I would be expected to put to sleep. I didn't think I could handle that and my vet dream came to an end. Instead I took business courses and got a job in the local vet's office, setting up appointments and doing the bookwork. I work three days a week and every second Saturday. I get to see lots of animals and occasionally I get to care for them. I just don't have to make any of the tough decisions. Not at work.

Ironically, though, I married a farmer so I didn't escape. Those tough decisions followed me home. I might as well have opted for vet school. At least I'd be getting paid better.

When Mom came home the following weekend, I told her the story of the calf skin coat and the calf that never lived to feel its warmth.

"Remember what your grandfather used to say?" she asked.

"If you've got livestock, you've got deadstock," I answered.

"Well, I hope I don't have any deadstock when it's my turn to check the cows tonight," Mom said.

## ~ SANDRA ~

These days I could be packed in ice and still sweat. Certainly I don't need full winter gear on a January night that is positively balmy by normal Manitoba standards. I pull on a pair of light-weight nylon pants and push my arms into a ski jacket that once belonged to Susan before pulling on my work boots. I grab the heavy-duty flashlight sitting by the door and head out onto the doorstep.

Immediately the dog pokes its head out of the doghouse. When it sees me, it comes out, tail wagging. Three a.m. or p.m., it makes no difference. The dog is always ready to go.

Fog obscures my vision, making the tree branches dance with the side-to-side motion of the flashlight. I plod along the path to the corrals, wishing for the crisp squeaky crunch of cold snow beneath my feet. The snow instead is a sodden mass that squelches as I move through it.

Reaching the corral fence, I slide the flashlight under the bottom rail and climb over the top. Once on the other side, I stand still and watch the cows. At first they are just shapes in the dim light sifting through the fog tendrils. Gradually, the shapes assume colour and become real.

Home for the weekend, I think it only fair that I give Dave some respite from the barnyard. The farm invested in a video surveillance system years ago and Dave and I can watch the television screen from inside the comfort of the house. But the TV cannot completely replace an actual walk through the corrals; always there is activity in the far corners of the enclosure that no camera can reach.

Only cows are in this enclosure; all the bulls are kept in a separate location. Males have no role in this place of pain and placentas. It reminds me of biblical times when women retired to the "red tent" once a month during their periods and during labour and childbirth. This is their red tent, open to the air and consecrated in the blood of birth.

Once a cow appears close to delivery, it is moved to what we affectionately call the maternity pen. We can easily view the pen on the television screen.

When the calf is born, mother and child are moved inside the barn where the newborn calf can find its legs and its mother's teats in insulated comfort. The pair remain inside for several days until the calf is well on its way before being led once more out to the larger enclosure.

I begin to walk towards the herd, using the flashlight to guide me over the lumps of semi-frozen straw and manure. The swaying light creates moving shadows. The dog, never one to miss a good chase, begins swinging left and right, yipping at the edges of the shadows.

The cattle take notice. Those lying down stand up. Those standing begin to move. Herd instincts take over and suddenly the cows are a moving mass. All it takes is one leader.

The dog, well-intentioned but as usual misguided, dashes into action. Its bark reverberating, it rounds the cattle and moves them back in my direction. The lead cow snorts and begins a rapid if clumsy gallop across the enclosure.

"Blue, stop!" I yell. To its credit, the dog obeys. But it is too late to stop the cows. And the light from my industrial strength flashlight seems to blind them, so that they lose themselves to panic. They charge in the direction of the light.

Fear paralyzes me for a few seconds, although it seems like longer. Then I turn and head back to the fence, scrambling, feet stumbling, to grasp the upper rail and safety. In my haste I drop the flashlight and it sends a thin line of light in the direction of the cattle.

My heart is pounding; I can feel its heaviness inside my chest. I sit and watch the cows race towards the far end of the corral, then turn and come back again.

Just be quiet, I tell myself. Give them time to calm down. It is the first time this winter I have been out to check on them. They have to get used to me again. Just be quiet and still.

I picture Dave watching my antics on the television in the house, although I know that he is asleep in our bed.

This is my turn to mind the cows, not his. Still I can imagine his laughter as clearly as if he was sitting in front of the television set and I was standing beside him.

The echoes of that unheard merriment anger me briefly, but the emotion subsides as quickly as it flared. Now it is my turn in front of the television screen. I watch myself running across the corrals. A middle-aged woman, never in the best of physical shape and certainly far from it now, hurtling across the mushy cow turds with terror written in the lines of her face. That final undignified scramble up the fence almost demands laughter. I obey, if somewhat ruefully.

The sound of my laughter alerts the cattle once more, but there is no sudden movement among the herd. From my perch I watch them, looking at the same time for signs of incipient labour. I can find none. In a few minutes, once I feel confident again, I will venture down from the fence and resume my walkabout.

I always feel at home within this female place. It is a place of waiting, I think. The waiting is by and large a peaceful time, albeit with the intrusions of humans and dogs. Cats, too. I watch as an orange barn cat makes its way through the herd towards me. When it gets to the fence, it leaps upwards, nimble as only cats can be, and curls itself in my lap. Once comfortable, it immediately begins to purr. The purring calms me.

The cows are calming down as well. Some are already lying down. Others have stopped by the bale feeder to eat.

Later in the season as January turns to February and February to March, young calves will leap about the enclosure with spring inside their bodies. They will be ready then to leave their mothers for longer periods of time in order to explore their surroundings.

At fifty-eight, I have no longing to be pregnant again, nor to face the demands of a young infant. I feel relief that my own children are long past that stage. Jon is himself a parent and Susan is in her own waiting place these days. Only Sam remains unattached and unfettered. How then to explain this ache?

The cycle of life has died inside my body. My periods once served as a kind of alarm clock with their regularity. Now months go by unheeded. How often I had welcomed them. Thank you, God. You love me, you really love me. Should one be flippant when thanking God? Perhaps not. Truth was, they called it the curse, but sometimes— oftentimes—it was a blessing. And yet—always the disclaimer—how often, too, I had seen with dismay the telltale stains. Another month, another failure. Make me fertile, Lord. Did I want to be pregnant? How I answered that question determined whether the period's arrival was good or bad news. And the answer changed from month to month, year to year.

All those years, more than forty of them, all those dollars spent on feminine protection. For a while when I was in my late 40s and early 50s, Dave would tease me whenever I came home with a jumbo package of maxi pads.

"You're optimistic, aren't you?" he asked. "Do you think you'll need them?"

"Hope springs eternal," I would answer.

In the end, he was right. I have an almost full package in the house and it sits gathering dust bunnies in the bathroom closet. Being prepared has its own price tag.

Beyond the paraphernalia of womanhood, there is the ritual. Months, years, entire decades are measured in menstrual cycles. I read in one of my textbooks that the origins of seeding and the harvest—the birth of agriculture—came from the twenty-eight-day cycle that governed both the moon and the female body. How does a woman measure time without the cycle of her body to guide her?

"With a calendar, of course," I can hear my husband saying. "I think you're taking these Women's Studies of yours way too seriously, Sandra."

Looking out at the pen of pregnant and nursing females, I wonder, not for the first time, whether cows go through menopause. I do not know the answer.

I have Googled bovine menopause on the Internet. I found hundreds of thousands of references for bovine, hundreds of thousands more for menopause, and nothing for the two words in combination. I did however find one scientific treatise detailing how hormonal changes associated with aging in women were similar to those experienced by cows. The bovine model is thus an appropriate one for further research and analysis into aging in human females, the paper said. Now that is an interesting thought.

I lift the cat off my lap and lower myself back onto the ground. The flashlight still has enough juice to let me see—just—the far end of the corral. I search for Greta, a twelve-year-old purebred who has elder status in the herd even though she is not this year in calf. Dave wanted to sell Greta last fall. A lifespan of thirteen or fourteen years is optimum for domestic cattle; he thought it was time for her to go. But our daughter Susan pled to keep the animal on the farm one more year and Dave relented. After only a few moments, I find the cow standing beside the water trough.

Cows that fail to conceive, such as Greta, are called dry cows. It seems an appropriate word. Sex is wet. Childbirth is wet. What better choice for a lack of either than the antonym.

Years ago Susan wanted to set up a retirement home for cows, bulls, and 4-H steers. A place where the pastures were lush and green and where water ran freely. A place where old age could creep up on them so slowly and softly they would welcome its soothing touch. A kind of bovine heaven on earth.

"It's a nice idea," Dave said at the time. "But where would you get the money to feed all those geriatric animals?"

Economics, the enemy of philanthropic foolishness. Not to mention youthful dreams.

One cow, a solid red colour except for the white blaze on her forehead, walks towards the fence. This cow's name is Annie. They all have names. Annie stops a few feet away and sniffs in the direction of my mittens.

"That's right, girl. Come smell the old lady," I say, extending my left arm. Annie backs away at first, but as the outstretched hand remains in position, she edges closer. Her wet nose touches the fabric of the mitten.

"See, Annie, you know me," I say. With my right hand, I pat the animal's neck. A second cow comes forward and then a third.

"You all want attention, don't you? I guess this means it's time for me to get back to work. Come on, girls, let's go."

Indeed I have spent too much time out here already.

Dave might wake and, finding me missing, come out to see what is taking me so long. He might hear my words and I know with the familiarity that comes from thirty-plus years of marriage what he will make of it.

"Do you know what menopause is?" he will ask, the expression in his eyes belying the tone of his voice. "It's hot flashes, mood swings, and women talking to cows."

He's behind the times. It's post-menopause, not menopause. But as long as he doesn't talk about facial hair, I will forgive him.

~ SUSAN ~

Carol had her baby on January 23, a little girl as expected. In the hospital the next afternoon, I found my friend nursing her daughter in a bedside armchair.

"Mommy love," I laughed as I placed the pink flower arrangement I had brought alongside three others already there.

"You'll see," she told me. "I had no idea what it was going to feel like until I had my first one. Although," she went on, as she moved her new baby from one breast to another, "there are apparently some women who don't feel that way."

"Really?" I asked. "I thought it was instinct that we love our babies."

"There are exceptions. Perhaps some women are just not cut out to be mothers. Or there could be other factors at play—depression, for example—which interferes with the normal bonding process."

I had never thought of that. I worried about being a good mother, never that I wouldn't love my child. It came as a shock that there was any question about it.

Suddenly I felt incredibly stupid. I didn't have a clue what I was getting myself into. Watching Carol position the baby's mouth more securely around her nipple, I felt panic rise inside me. How the hell was I going to pull this off?

Carol and Bill named their baby Samantha, which amused me since that is our cat's name. But it reminded us that we had better get thinking about a name for our own child.

I found Lachlan in my book and suggested it to Glen.

"It's Gaelic, means land of the lakes."

"Sounds kinda out there to me," he said. "How about my dad's name? Joseph."

"But then we'd have to call him Joseph David or David Joseph. We couldn't just name the baby after one grandfather. It would have to be both."

I had already looked up David in the name book, of course. It means "beloved." And Joseph means "God will increase." Apparently our fathers are biblically blessed.

My mother-in-law, too. Joan means "God is gracious." Only my mother's name has no religious undertones; Sandra is a feminine form of Alexander and means "defender of men." Or "unheeded prophetess." I thought she would prefer the latter.

"And what if it's a girl?" Glen asked.

"Good question. I don't know."

For some reason, my mind couldn't settle on a girl's name, couldn't even settle on the idea of seeking a girl's name. I would open my ancient name book or search for modern equivalents on the Internet, but somehow always ended up in the male section. Wishful thinking? Psychic powers? Was there a little penis in my belly making itself felt?

When people asked me whether I wanted a boy or a girl, I told them that it didn't matter to me. Traditionally, I suppose, farm families blessed the arrival of a son since sons would carry on the family business. Sons were a way of ensuring the work would continue. But that's not quite true anymore. Look at my family. Two boys and neither of them are farmers, at least not full time. The man's role has changed, no longer protector and provider, the new role not yet certain.

Yet girls still have to fight for our place at the trough and we can fight dirty. I think it is because as soon as there are two of us in a room our hormones start competing. Our periods synchronize; ever notice that? And it doesn't matter what the difference in our ages might be; the mother-daughter thing means nothing in biology. Perhaps that is subconsciously why I would prefer a son. So that I can have one of those special mother-son bonds, instead of one of those complicated mother-daughter ones. I think that mothers and daughters spend whole lifetimes trying to figure out what they want from each other.

Maybe if I were one of those women who couldn't wait to dress her daughter in pink frills, it would be different. I'm not one of those women.

I think that Glen would make a good dad for a little girl, though. Father-daughter is special. I want that for him and for our daughter if we have one.

# EIGHT

*My name is Susan and I am in labour. I am eight centimetres dilated.*

*Focus. Things that come in eights. Legs on a spider. Hot dog and hamburger buns. Sides on a stop sign. Crayons in a box, a standard box. Hours in a good night's sleep. Legs on an octopus. Behind the eight ball. Pieces of eight. A figure eight. A magic eight ball. A card game called Crazy Eights. An eight turned on its side is the Greek symbol for infinity. Who would want to do this over and over and over again?*

Lynne and I went for lunch one day in early February. I had come into town for a doctor's appointment.

Lynne looked awful. I don't think I had ever seen her on a bad hair day before.

"What's wrong?" I asked after we had placed our orders.

"He's moving in with another woman," she said.

I took a few moments to absorb this news.

"That was quick," I said.

"No, you don't get it. He was planning it all the time. That's why he left his wife."

"So you weren't the 'other woman' after all? You were the other 'other woman'?"

Lynne started to cry and got up from the table. She walked towards the washrooms.

I had recently seen a movie about multiple other women, all of them ganging up on the man who had juggled them successfully for a surprisingly long time. It was a comedy but I knew Lynne wouldn't find any humour in the reference. I was still trying to figure out what to say when Lynne returned, her features composed once more. At the same time the waitress arrived with our salads.

"I feel so stupid, Susan. Here I was thinking he left her for me, when it wasn't me at all. I was just a diversion while he got his ducks in a row for his life with someone else. I was actually thinking about leaving Brian."

That would have surprised me six months ago. It didn't now, although I am not sure she would ever have gone through with it. Thinking about is different than doing.

I don't remember falling in love with Glen. It was a slow slide rather than an abrupt descent. Before we were lovers, we were friends and we shared a love for the farm and our animals. Being with Glen has always seemed right to me, as if we're two jigsaw pieces with interlocking edges. We fit.

"So what are you going to do now?" I asked.

"I don't know. I would like to yell and scream at him. I want to tell his new woman what he was doing. I wish I had never met him."

If Lynne did make a scene, if she told the new woman that her man had been a bad boy, what would be the cost? Had she left a husband, too? Were there other women? How many families were implicated? It was too complicated for me. Give me my cows any day. They may not be monogamous but they don't have to worry about ethics either.

The mature cows had started calving earlier that week. The night before my lunch date with Lynne, I had gone out to the barn in time to witness a cow placidly consuming her placenta, calf resting on the straw beside her.

Occasionally, a cow might not eat her placenta, but most of the time she does. Not sure why. Perhaps she is just hungry and it is conveniently nearby. Perhaps it contains some nutrients that she needs. I've read that it might be a way of hiding the evidence of the birth, some primordial defence mechanism against predators, which might smell the newborn. But maybe it's just instinct.

When I was taking my business administration course in Winnipeg, I met a girl whose cousin had adopted a back-to-the-earth lifestyle in Hawaii. She married there and had a child. Part of the birthing ritual was a ceremony in which the placenta was buried in a sacred space. The family back in Manitoba was shocked.

I understand there are cultures in which cooked placenta is considered a delicacy. I also understand that placenta, both ruminant and human, is used in the cosmetic industry. I am not tempted by any of it, although my squeamishness seems silly to me.

I was squeamish about a lot of things; I blamed it on the pregnancy. Glen shot a magpie one morning and the bloody streak across a snowbank made me gag. Glen was proud. If you know anything about magpies, you know that they are not easy to shoot. This was the first time he had ever managed it.

Magpies are pests. They feed on manure and the insects that can be found in manure. They also forage for ticks and other insects on the backs of domestic animals. They pick at open wounds and scabs on the backs of livestock until they create a much larger wound that may eventually become infected and, in some instances, even kill the animal. Like ravens, magpies may peck the eyes out of newborn or sick livestock.

To add insult to injury, they steal the dog food right out of the bowl and they are quite brazen about it. That's what did this one in.

But they are striking birds, especially when the black of their wings appears an iridescent blue and green in the sunshine. Nature gave them good looks to balance their bad behaviour.

We hadn't seen as many magpies this winter as we usually do. In fact, local birdwatchers who had participated in the annual Christmas Day bird count reported lower numbers in many of the species that are commonly found in the area. One theory was that there were fewer birds because there were fewer cattle and therefore less grain pickings for the birds. There would also be less grain to attract mice. The fewer the mice, the fewer the predatory birds like owls and hawks.

The last decade has been hard on cattle producers and many have sold their herds. They've given up. Perhaps someday science will point the finger at cattle farmers for reducing their herds and lowering bird populations as a result. When we sell our animals, we take down the welcome sign for the birds. On the other hand, if we keep our herd or add to it, we get called on everything from methane gas production to e-coli contamination. Damned if we do and damned if we don't. I'm getting paranoid.

I just want to take care of my animals and feed people.

We got a late night call on Valentine's Day.

"Your grandmother died," Dad said.

Dad's mother was eighty-eight years old. She lived in her own home until she was eighty-three and then moved to a senior's facility in town. She had had a massive heart attack that evening.

*Grandma, I'm sorry I never liked your name. My name. I would take that back if I could. My regret is sharp and surprising.*

Mom came home when she got the news. She loved Grandma. They could easily have been mother and daughter. I'm not sure I will ever feel the same way about my mother-in-law. Wish I could. It would be nice to have two mothers.

Sam flew home, too; Dad drove into the city to meet his flight the day before the funeral. Grandma always called my youngest brother "Little Sam," even when he grew taller than both Dad and Jon. I guess the babies of a family are always babies in some ways. And Sam was very fond of Grandma. Not that all three of us weren't fond of her, because we were, very much so. It's just that Sam seemed to have a special relationship with her.

Grandma never intruded even though we pretty much lived in the same yard. She respected boundaries, although she would never have phrased it in those words. She was different than Grandpa, whose definition of boundaries stopped at the fence line. Grandma never gave her opinion unless it was requested; Grandpa always gave his whether it was requested or not. In fact, he was twice as likely to voice it if you didn't want to hear it.

Grandma had told us often that she wanted a traditional burial. Grandpa was buried in a coffin in one of the local cemeteries, and she would be, too. She feared cremation because of the possibility that she could still be alive when the furnace doors opened. It was one of the few things my very practical grandma could be irrational about. She had her reasons. When she was a child, she had heard stories about scarlet fever victims in New Iceland who slipped into a deep coma and were pronounced dead, only to revive a day later. She told us about ropes that extended from the coffin to a bell on a pole beside the grave so that the revived corpse could alert the community. I'm alive, I'm alive. Get me out of here! Cremains cannot shout. Therefore she preferred to remain a corpse. There were many holes in this argument, not the least of which being that a body emptied of all bodily fluids and filled with formaldehyde wasn't likely to shout either, but Grandma vigorously defended her position.

It was a large funeral, standing room only in the United Church in town. In movies and on television, you watch funerals at which the mourners number less than ten. I find that alien and sad: alien because I have never been to a funeral that small and sad because, I'm not sure why. Perhaps because so few people mark the end of someone's life, although surely that life intersected with more than eight or nine others. Where is the family? Where is the community? What would it be like to be so alone?

There were many people at Grandma's funeral whom I did not recognize, even though I suspected they might be related to me. There were others who were not family, but who had come home to reconnect with community members as they mourned the loss of one of their own. In many ways, it was like a reunion, a way of solidifying even temporarily the bonds of blood and shared history.

We sang "Softly and tenderly Jesus is calling" and "The Old Rugged Cross," the old standbys as my mother calls them. Actually that's what Grandma was. An old standby.

She had been pleased to learn that I was pregnant. Motherhood, she believed, was both a woman's duty and pleasure. Sex, on the other hand, was weighted more on the duty side. "Your grandfather liked it," she said once, as if accepting him in bed was akin to cooking his favourite meal, a favour for the man she lived with.

*Oh Grandma, I miss you. I don't know how you lived with Grandpa all those years without some of that cantankerousness rubbing off on you.*

Dad's oldest sister gave the eulogy. Dad has three sisters and he is the youngest in the family. There was never any doubt that he would eventually take over the family farm. This was an era when daughters were never considered farmer material, even though if they married one, they would be expected to do all manner of farm chores.

Things were different now. It's just as likely to be a daughter as a son who wants to farm. But parents cannot afford to give the farm away and children cannot afford to pay what it is worth. When Dad decides to quit, the farm will most likely be sold.

In the eulogy, my aunt talked about Grandma's skills as a farmer's wife and mother. Why are we always defined by our relationships with others, I wondered. If anyone deserved to be valued for herself, it was my grandma.

When I was younger, we had a collie at home. I found her one day on the side of the road lying in a pool of vomit, motionless but still alive. She died a few minutes later. I had never seen anything or anyone die before. One minute she was our dog, the next she was something that resembled our dog but yet wasn't. I didn't know how to explain it.

Later Dad said he thought she must have eaten something poisonous. I ran to Grandma's house and thrust myself against her. "My dog is dead," I cried.

"Shhh," she said, holding my head against her quite ample chest. "All things have their time, my girl."

At first I was upset with her for calling my dog a thing. Eventually I figured out that she wasn't just talking about dogs or people. She was talking about everything.

Grandma was like an oak tree with its roots so firmly planted it couldn't move far. But it could reach with its branches and its roots stretched in every direction far below where no one could see.

Those roots were her strength. Death was a stroke of lightning.

Once when I was picking Saskatoons I came across a poplar tree with a swash of red fabric tied around its trunk. I didn't realize at first what it was until Glen explained it to me. I had heard about it before, but this was the first time I had seen it for myself.

We live not far from a First Nations reserve. When a First

Nations person dies, those who grieve may select a tree in his memory. The fabric wrapped around the trunk may be from an item of clothing once worn by the deceased or perhaps it might be his favourite colour. The tree is readily identified by its sash and can be visited as others might visit a grave. The idea being, I suppose, that the spirit lives on in living things. Perhaps I could borrow from a culture that is not mine and pick a tree for my grandma. I would like it to be an oak tree, but I suppose any kind of tree might do.

The funeral service was followed by interment at the same cemetery where my grandfather was buried. It was a grey day and, although the temperature was seasonal, the wind sliced through me. I shivered in the winter coat that refused to close around my belly and Glen put an arm around my shoulders.

Then back to the community hall in town for the lunch. Coffee and tea, towering plates of egg salad and ham sandwiches, bowls of pickles, more plates of cake and cookies. Funeral food. Sometimes I think that people come to funerals just for the food.

Grace said by the minister, eating and drinking, and then the line-up to greet family members. So sorry for your loss. She was a grand lady. Hugs from people I did not recognize. Finally we could go back to Mom and Dad's, where aunts, uncles, and cousins gathered for yet more coffee and food. A Tupperware container of leftovers had been thrust upon us as we left the hall.

Glen and I were the last to leave Mom and Dad's that evening and I helped Mom clear up the coffee cups and cake plates.

"Do you like university?" I asked her. It was the first time I had had a chance to talk to her about her new life.

"It's harder than I thought," she said. "It's a long time since I've been a student. I've forgotten how to study. But yes, I'm enjoying the courses. I'm looking at things in a new way."

"I'd forgotten how city people think of us," she added.

"They don't think of us at all."

"You're right, Susan. They don't."

"We know more about the city than the city knows about us."

"A smart mouse always keeps track of what the elephant is doing."

"I guess."

I grew bored with the conversation, brought it back to the family.

"I thought you were leaving Dad," I blurted out.

Mom stopped washing cutlery and looked at me.

"When you told us at Christmas, that's the first thing I thought."

"I see," she said. And then, "No, I wasn't planning that. In some ways I wasn't thinking of your dad at all. I just wanted to begin something new. Think about different things.

"This is my grand adventure," my mother said as she reached for another handful of coffee spoons.

"You wouldn't ever want to leave Dad, would you?"

"Well, you know, Susan, there are very few marriages, probably none at all, that don't go through bad times. Times when you look at the man you married and ask yourself, 'what am I doing here?' Times when he doesn't like you very much and you don't like him very much and it would be very easy to say to heck with it.

"But no, I'm not likely to leave your Dad, not voluntarily anyway. And I doubt that he would ever leave me. Even if sometimes we both wonder about what life might be like somewhere else. Everybody does. You get to a point in your life where you say 'Is this all there is?'"

It wasn't what I wanted to hear.

"I guess maybe Glen and I are lucky. We fit together," I said.

"Do you remember that farm puzzle you used to play with?" Mom asked.

I did. It had been Jon's originally and was handed down to me and then to Sam. Each heavy wooden piece featured a different farm animal. When you put the puzzle together, you had a farm scene. I loved that puzzle.

"Whatever happened to it?"

"It's upstairs in one of the closets. It's missing one piece—the pig, I think."

"So why have you kept it?"

Mom gave me this look that said I should be able to figure it out for myself. It annoyed me and we finished the dishes in silence.

Sam came up behind us, draping his arms around our shoulders.

"Aw, am I too late to help with the dishes?" he asked.

"Your timing is perfect," I said.


I had coffee with Sam early the next afternoon before his flight home.

"You're being kinda hard on Mom, aren't you?" he asked.

"What do you mean, hard on Mom?"

"Just because she wants to expand her horizons a little. This family is so tied to the land and its rituals. I don't blame her for wanting to see beyond that."

"You love the land, too."

"Yes, those roots pull you back. But I don't want to live here. You can bury me beside Grandma and Grandpa."

I shivered.

"You're being morbid."

"You live and then you die," he said and grinned.

Another of Grandpa's famous lines. They're never going to die as long as people keep repeating them.

"You know what, Susan? I think you hide yourself inside the barn so you don't have to deal with the big bad world."

"What a weird thing to say, Sam. I'm not hiding from it. I'm living in the thick of it, birth and death and everything in between."

"The world according to Moo," he said.

"Oh shut up," I answered, but my tone belied the words. Sam was the only person I knew who could make me want to laugh and swear at the same time.

Perhaps because he is the baby of the family, Sam is good at silliness.

"I think I like living in the midst of ordinary vices," I said. "No gang warfare, no organized crime, no terrorism."

"Ah, but the seeds of all that heavy duty stuff are in those ordinary vices you talk about," my little brother said.

"I'm glad you're here, even if it's just for a short time," I said. "You're one of the few people in the world that I can have this kind of conversation with."

"What kind of conversation?"

"Don't be obtuse. You know what I'm talking about. A conversation that isn't all about cattle and grain and farming and weather."

# NINE

*Things that come in nines. That's an easy one. Nine months of pregnancy. Nine planets in the solar system. Men Very Early Made Jars Stand Up Nearly Perpendicular. Mars Venus Earth Mercury Jupiter Saturn Uranus Neptune Pluto. Except now they say that Pluto might not be a planet. So maybe the planets belong to things that come in eights instead. But I will not go back there. Nine lives of a cat. Nine innings in a baseball game. Take me out to the ball game. Possession is nine points of the law. Cloud nine. Dressed to the nines. The whole nine yards.*

*Two, four, six, eight.*
*What will I appreciate?*
*When dilation gets to ten*
*Cuz I will never go this way again.*

*Ah, but women do, don't they? Mom told me that you forget the pain between pregnancies. If men had to give birth, she said, there would be zero population growth. Men don't forget as easily. I don't see how I could possibly forget.*

*I feel greasy and huge, my legs splayed out under a hospital-issue blanket. You're doing great, the nurses tell me. Glen says so, too. He doesn't know what else to say. Maybe he should go buy some more staples.*

March was difficult, full of spite and broken promises: a spring thaw and sunshine one day, snow and ice storms the next.

On nice days, I waddled out to the barnyard through grey mud that was soft and sludge-like beneath my boots. The young calves were quick on their newly-found feet. They ran and jumped around the corrals, then returned to their mothers for a feed and snuggle. When the baby kicked, I imagined him with that same joyous energy. My mother said I was going to have a boy because of the way I carried this child—straight out and to the front. That's a boy, she said.

The calves knew me by then. They no longer ran away when I approached. I patted them with my right hand while rubbing my belly with my left. Sometimes I would stretch an ungloved hand towards one and it would mistake my hand for a teat, latching on with vacuum-like strength.

One morning I let myself into the pen of the calving barn to see the newest arrival. The cow pricked up its ears and turned towards me, the whites of its eyes a blaze in the brown of its face. I barely had time to get out and latch the panels together before she was there, head lowered and nostrils flaring. If I hadn't had the chain lock in place, she would have head butted me.

"We need to get rid of that cow," I told Glen once my breathing had returned to normal. We had said the same thing last year. She was a docile creature for fifty weeks out of fifty-two, but when her calf was new, she became a warrior. It was one of the first things Dad taught me when I began working with the cattle at home. Bulls you never trust ever. Cows you never trust when they have young calves at foot. So what almost happened was my own fault; I should not have tried to enter the pen.

With another cow, however, it would not have been such a big deal. She would have watched me carefully, but probably would not have come near me unless I attempted to come near her calf.

This cow was different. For several weeks after the calf was born, she wasn't just protective. She was murderous. If there is a bovine equivalent of post-partum psychosis, she showed all the symptoms.

But her first calf had been one of the best in the herd last year and she was so quiet normally that we had forgotten her Jekyll and Hyde transformation.

"We have to sell her this year," Glen said. "We can't have a cow like that around the place now that there'll be little kids around."

I noticed that he said "kids" plural and thought he was rushing things a bit. Let's get this pregnancy over before you plan another one, I thought. Besides, it would be several years before our first child started exploring the barnyard on his own. But I knew what Glen meant. This cow had to go.

My father-in-law made a point of driving out to the farm almost daily. Although retired, he couldn't get over the habits of a lifetime, I guess. He had discovered caution in his senior years, especially after he suffered a stroke in his early sixties, and he didn't chance the semi-frozen and rutted corrals. Instead he drove up to the gate, opened the window, and watched from the safety and warmth of his vehicle. I could tell he wanted to get out there and touch some hides the way I did.

At the same time, I was amazed at how far he had come since his stroke. We all were.

~ JOAN ~

Wires stretch from my husband to machines beside the hospital bed. Coloured lights flicker on the front of the machines.

"What do the lights mean?" I ask the nurse.

But her answer does not help me much. I am not surprised. Both Joe and I have sisters who are nurses. Whenever the two of them talk shop, my internal remote switches channels. They speak a language I don't understand.

As far as I can figure out, the lights flicker because Joe's condition is not stable. And the appearance of red lights would be a bad thing, like a stop sign at the end of the road. Red lights would bring the medical staff running.

Joe's sleep is restless, broken by guttural noises and gasps for air. His face seems foreign, inert and plastic, the features melting one into the other. When I cover his hand with mine, there is no response.

The doctor on call told me that Joe had a stroke and asked about the family medical history. His mother died of a heart attack, I told the doctor. His father died of cancer. You don't ever beat the big C, Joe used to say. We were having a late night cup of tea before bed.

"First thing in the morning," Joe started to say and I knew before the sentence was completed what the words were going to be. First thing in the morning we would move the cattle from one paddock to another.

But the words did not come and I looked up from the cup I was spooning sugar into. Joe's face was skewed; his mouth moved but there was no sound. I stood up to go to him but could not get there fast enough to halt his slide to the floor.

I called 9-1-1. Joe hates ambulances. I was sure he would tell me to hang up the phone. No need for that, I expected him to say. He said nothing.

I could have ridden in the ambulance, but I said that no, I would bring the car. If I didn't bring a vehicle, how would I get home? But in the forty-five minutes it took to get to the emergency ward, I wished I had made a different choice. The closer we got to the hospital, the more convinced I became that Joe had died with only the ambulance attendant beside him. I watched the ambulance attendants roll Joe's stretcher into the emergency entrance and tried to get up the courage to follow them inside.

I remembered the cows in the west pasture, the ones that Joe, I was sure, had intended to move in the morning. First thing when I get home, I told myself. Poor things will be hungry. They had eaten the grass down to its roots. With that purpose, I felt strong enough to leave the car.

Emergency was busy. Blood soaked the fabric wound around a man's hand.

"I was trying to unplug the lawn mower," I heard the man say.

"Can you help my wife?" another man asked. "She got stung and she's allergic."

A bone was sticking out of a young boy's arm. He stared at it with fascination, while his mother talked to the nurses.

They wouldn't let me see Joe. "Wait out here," they said. "We'll come for you."

I called Lynne. "Your dad had a stroke," I told her.

"Is he going to be all right?"

"I don't know. Please come as soon as you can."

Glen had gone fishing with a group of friends. Cell phone reception up there is non-existent.

By the time Lynne and Brian arrive, Joe has been moved to a bed in ICU. The nurse has set up a cot for me, but I cannot sleep. I blame it on the blinking lights. I am afraid to close my eyes in case they turn red.

"Mom," Lynne says, and I stand up to hug her. The nurse brings more chairs and the three of us settle down to watch and wait. What's that they say? Hurry up and wait.

"I talked to the nurse outside," Brian says, reaching for my hand. "She says it's serious."

Hours later, as daylight peeks through the vertical blinds in the room's one window, three doctors come in, the doctor I had seen before and two strangers. They examine Joe's chart and fiddle with the machines. They line themselves up in front of us. "I'm sorry," the tallest one says. "This could go either way. It was a massive stroke."

"But there is still a chance he could pull through?" Lynne asks.

"Yes. But it would be wise to face the possibility that he won't. I'm sorry."

I want our family doctor, but they tell us that he is on vacation, returning later this week. Dr. Carter would touch me on the shoulder, spreading sympathy and strength with his fingers.

The doctors depart with assurances that they will continue to monitor Joe closely and promises to answer any questions we might have. The blinking lights, coloured eyes in a mechanical face, have given me a headache.

"I'm going home," I say, standing up and reaching for my purse and car keys.

"But aren't you going to wait here for Dad to wake up?" Lynne asks.

"You can wait with him," I say. "The cattle in the west pasture need to be moved. Your dad and I were going to do it this morning. If he wakes up, tell him where I am."

"I think you should stay with us, Mom," Brian says. "I could go if you'd like, and you can stay with Lynne."

"No, I would like to go by myself," I say. "I need to do this. I'll be back as soon as I can."

I leave the machines behind.

The headache recedes as soon as I get in the car. There are cumulous clouds in the blue sky. Nothing bad can happen on such a day, I tell myself. I wish. My mom died on a sunny day. My daughter was born during a snowstorm. We farmers think that weather controls our lives, but in life's most important moments, it is irrelevant.

About halfway home, there is a vacant farmyard. The

two-storey house is grey and weathered, no glass in the windows, roof sagging. The house has been there as long as I can remember. There used to be outbuildings as well, but over time they were vandalized or just fell down of their own accord. I have always been curious about the family who farmed that land and lived in that house. I know they left in the 1950s, selling the land to farmers who had no need for the yard site. I even know their name was Moffat and that they moved to another province where one of their adult children lived. But I know nothing about the memories inside those four walls. I do not know how the rooms were furnished, or what family dramas played out there. In my imagination, I cover the chesterfield and armchair with crocheted doilies, fill the pantry with raisin pies and place a ceramic pitcher beside the wash bowl in the bathroom.

I like to make up stories about this and other houses, but realize now that I have never imagined vacant a house that Joe and I once lived in.

As I drive past our driveway, I remember the dog has not been fed yet this morning. So I stop, back up, and drive into the yard. The Border Collie comes rushing out from behind the barn, yipping loudly, tail held high. How often have I seen that black and white streak and thought "skunk" before realizing it is our dog. He isn't moving as quickly as he used to; arthritis and age are taking their toll. How quickly age catches us, I think.

When I bring the dog a plate, he comes up beside me and waits until I turn away before lowering his head to the food. Strange dog. He has always demanded privacy at meal times.

The tea cups are still on the kitchen table and I carry them to the sink; I consider washing them but decide against it. They can wait.

The cattle see me as soon as I park at the gate. They follow me across the pasture to another fence. You let the cattle into a small paddock, leave them to graze it down and then move them again. The experts tell us it is an environmentally sound practice, but it just seems like common sense to me. Common sense is undervalued these days; at least until scientific research data proves it true. Then it's gospel. The old becomes new and then old again.

I unlatch the gate and open it wide. The cattle come, even without me calling to them.

At the end of the line comes the bull, more than a ton of mature testosterone in a leather hide. The bull moves strongly, scrotal sac swinging back and forth between its hind legs.

"Good bulls die young," I can hear Joe saying. A variation on the paving of paradise. You don't know what you've got till it's gone. Or Murphy's Law, perhaps. The good die young, the mediocre stumble on.

Only after several years does a bull's genetic inheritance make itself known in its progeny. This one has proven himself over time while managing to avoid the pitfalls of illness or accident.

Years ago we spent thousands of dollars on a yearling bull with a pedigree to match its price tag. Joe wanted that bull so badly, its purchase a symbolic measure of the farm's success, and we were all proud of it. Lynne posted photographs on the farm website. We got one year's worth of calves out of that bull, but it died in its third year. The autopsy showed a massive internal infection. The one set of calves he sired contained many keepers and we still have cows in the herd that we can trace back to him. But we have never again spent that kind of money on any animal.

If Joe were here, he would be calling to the cattle. Cows cows cows. The words would hang in the air like boldface capitals, fading as they fell to lower case letters in a smaller font.

I always tell Joe that he doesn't need to yell to get their attention. We don't need to chase them. We can just take our time and they will do what we want. It is what they want, too. Who doesn't want the green grass on the other side of the fence? Or water when the trough is dry? Feed them and they will come is not just for people. With one to lead, the rest will follow.

Sometimes, though, the animals do not understand the rationale behind human directions. They will balk or suddenly move at right angles. It is then that Joe's impatience shows. It is almost always guaranteed to cause friction between us, him yelling at me for being too slow or not in the right place at the right time, me yelling at him for being in such a hurry.

But you can't wait, can you, Joe? Move the cattle so we can get on with the haying. Finish the haying so we can take out the bulls. Take out the bulls so we can wean the calves. Your life is the work and the work is the cattle.

Joe has followed me here, I think. I can hear his words even if I cannot see him.

When his dad was undergoing cancer treatments, Joe spent more time outdoors on the farm than ever. The kids joke about so-called happy places. The farm was Joe's happy place. His hiding place, too. He hid from his father's death there.

More than forty years we have been married and we have never been away from the farm for more than three days in a row. Joe gets nervous when he isn't at home. He worries that something might go wrong without his supervision. His misses the morning light through our east bedroom window.

"We've been gone long enough," he says. "Let's go home."

We are always good house guests; we never outstay our welcome.

Joe was delighted that Glen wanted to farm, continuing the link to the land that is several generations deep. Granted, Glen's preference is grain farming. He doesn't share his dad's love for cattle, at least not to the same extent. But at least he is devoted to the land itself. Farming without that passion is unwise. You have nothing to sustain your spirit when things go wrong. And Susan's enthusiasm for her animals is more than enough to make up for any shortage on Glen's side. The farm will be in good hands when they get married and take over.

I already recognized Joe's passion when I started dating him. We'd start each summer evening with a truck ride to check the cattle. And after we were married, the boundaries between house and farm blurred. Both are home.

I remember once a cow died giving birth in January and we knew the calf would not make it without heat. So we brought it into the house, laid it on blankets on the kitchen floor and rubbed it down with towels until the chill was gone from its young hide. We kept it inside until the next day when it had enough strength to find its legs and wobble unsteadily to its feet. Lynne decided we should call it Wobbly and Wobbly she was until the day she died ten years later. If I close my eyes, I can see Joe and Lynne kneeling on the floor beside that calf.

"Is she going to be all right, Dad?"

"She's going to be just fine, Lynne."

Such confidence in his voice, something a daughter could wrap around her shoulders to keep her warm. I could use that confidence now.

We never discussed what we would do if work became impossible, did we, Joe? But I can imagine the conversation. "Let me go," you would say. No heroics. At least I think that is what you would say. Perhaps I am fooling myself. Perhaps it is me who would say those words while you would want to continue the fight. I am confused. I do not know. Why did we never talk about it? Were we afraid? I'm afraid now.

"Can you hear me, Joe? I'm talking to you."

The cows are drinking at the pit. I close the gate and walk back to the car.

I am almost there when the cell rings. It is Lynne.

"Is there any change?"

"No," she says. "Where are you, Mom? It seems to be taking you a long time."

"I'm just about to drive back," I tell her. "I moved the cows and watched them for a bit. Counted them. Dad and I were going to do that together this morning."

"Yes, you said that," my daughter says. "So you're coming right back?"

"Yes, getting into the car now." And to prove the point, I open the driver's door.

"All right, see you soon," she says. "Susan was able to get hold of Glen. He'll be here in a few hours."

"Good," I say. "We can all be together."

"Mom?"

"Yes?"

"Are you all right?"

"I'm fine, Lynne."

I am the child telling lies to her parent.

~ SUSAN ~

Joe surprised everyone, most of all the pessimistic doctors, by recovering from his stroke. When he regained consciousness, his first words were garbled and anxious.

"Did you move the cattle?" he asked. Joan assured him that she had. He sank back into a more natural sleep and the doctors said he had turned the corner. It was not an overnight recovery, more a slow and steady progress towards some kind of normalcy. Not quite what it had been, but closer.

It wasn't easy for Joe to move to town, even though he accepted the good judgment behind the decision. But a man on his deathbed who still worries about feeding the cattle doesn't leave the farm behind when he leaves the yard.

That's one of the reasons why I flared up a few days ago when I read a newspaper article telling farmers to leave their emotions out of it when making business plans.

"Listen to this crap," I said to Glen and read the entire article to him.

"Easier said than done," he said.

I guess anyone who owned a family business would find it hard to walk away. Especially if the business had been in the family for several generations.

The list on the fridge was messy with crossed out lines and scribbles. Near the top of the list, my nephews had drawn a stork carrying a baby in a diaper, with the words Wah Wah Wah issuing from the infant's mouth. The bottom of the diaper was worked in with brown crayon, an indication that our baby had enjoyed his first bowel movement on the flight. Their mother had not been pleased with them.

- ~~Crib~~ and/or cradle (J&J)
- ~~Sheets and towels and baby facecloths~~
- ~~Receiving blankets~~
- ~~Diapers and a diaper bag~~
- ~~Car seat (bucket)~~
- Baby bouncer
- ~~Sleepers~~
- ~~Onesies~~ Twosies Threesies Foursies (My nephews again)
- Change table
- High chair
- ~~Baby bathtub~~
- ~~Soothers~~
- ~~Rattles~~
- Breast pump

The change table and high chair were coming as family gifts; Joan and Joe were giving us a crib. I still hadn't got around to that damn breast pump, but I promised myself I would pick one up before I started mat leave.

Our senses of smell returned with the thaw when it came. Frozen things have no aroma, but the warm sun made the barnyard pungent once again. When I returned to the house, I lifted my hands to my nose and sniffed the calf smell that lingered there. I hated to wash it off.

Cows are motherhood in a leather hide, I thought. Pregnancy made me feel like my cows: bulging stomach, awkward and ungainly gait, swollen udders with distended veins visible beneath the skin.

Now it was time to start introducing the heifers, and select cows, to the male of the species. When we saw that the female was in heat, we would bring her in with a specially selected male.

Dad, who is a trained AI technician, used to inseminate cows artificially on the farm. He would manually insert bull semen into a cow when she was in heat.

Frozen semen is thawed and put inside a special insemination gun. When the farmer noticed that a cow was in heat, he would immediately call his AI tech. Insemination must be done twelve to twenty-four hours after the animal goes into heat to ensure that the sperm arrives at the fertilization site a few hours before ovulation.

Apparently AI was originally used because there was less chance of injury to the cow with an insemination gun than with a raging bull. Buying the semen is less expensive than feeding and caring for a bull all year long. And semen can be tested for a sexually-treated disease that a herd bull could unknowingly transmit.

And finally, you get to breed your cow to a quality bull with the traits you are looking for. It's all win-win as far as I can see.

I have been trying to persuade Glen to get a few more purebreds so that we can try some AI breeding, but so far at least he hasn't been enthusiastic. I'm going to keep working on him. I'd be willing to take the training so that I could do the AI work myself.

In the meantime, we're doing it the old-fashioned way. We put the boy and girl together, and watch for signs that sex has occurred. When we notice that the cow's tail is held out at a crooked angle or that there is fluid discharge from her vulva, we release the animals and send them back to their pens. A cow's cycle is about twenty-one days, so if she shows signs of being in heat again three weeks after the mating, you know you have to try again.

It's rather like being a peeping tom, keeping an eye on our cattle to see if they've engaged in sex or not. Bovine voyeurism, I call it.

Once last winter Glen accidentally put the wrong bull in with a heifer, wrong because they both had the same mother. It was equivalent to having sex with your half-sibling. The bull was good to mate with heifers, but not this particular one, and Glen never thought of their shared bloodline. When I got home from work and realized what he had done, I was angry.

"Sorry, Sus," he said. "I don't remember those things as well as you do."

The heifer bore a bull calf a few weeks ago and we made it into a steer. There was nothing identifiably wrong with the animal, but it had to be designated for slaughter because of the risk its genetic makeup posed to the herd.

It made me wonder about our baby, what traits he or she would be born with, what strengths and weaknesses, what potential, what risks. All determined by one egg and one sperm from two separate donors united for a lifetime by one act of coitus. More to it than the shape of a nose or the colour of one's hair. Hidden things that might never show at all, or might suddenly erupt in crisis. Scary stuff. Or wonderful surprises. Who knew which?

Glen's family is all on the tall side; his dad is an angular man with wide shoulders, his mother thin with short blonde hair that has faded to a pale gray. Lynne inherited that hair colour and Glen's is a darker blonde. My family is both shorter and heavier, although none of us are what you would call overweight. Jon would come the closest. We all have dark hair and my brothers inherited my mother's natural wave, although on them it shows as a tousled look that I rather like. Mom has coloured her hair for years now and says she does not want to know how grey it is underneath.

I went for afternoon coffee with two of my co-workers, Karen and Diane, on one of those unpleasant March days, the wind a wet chill on our skin and the earlier thaw only an icy memory.

"Did I hear Brian and Lynne went to the Dominican for a week?" Karen asked me.

"Yep," I said. "They pulled the kids out of school and all five of them went."

"Kinda strange to take the kids with them to the

Dominican, isn't it? I mean, it's more of a couples' destination."

"Maybe they needed the kids to run interference between them."

I regretted the words the minute they came out of my mouth, even though it was exactly what I had thought when I first heard about the trip.

"What do you mean, interference? Is there trouble in paradise?"

"Susan has dirt on Lynne, don't you, Susan?" This from Diane.

I denied it and said no more, but the damage was done. I had planted the seeds that would become a rumour.

But when the bombshell hit, I never saw it coming.

We woke one morning to news on the radio that a BSE-infected cow had been found in Alberta. Now one cow does not make an epidemic and one cow is not enough to close borders. Not yet anyway. But it did make us ask the question "What if?"

And it wrecked an until-then perfectly fine winter morning.

Glen went uptown to join the local coffee clutch at the gas station. There would be lots of discussion there about the issue, I knew. And many solutions suggested, some of them not politically correct. Those who cried wolf would cry some more and so it would go, one cup of coffee after another.

When he came home for lunch, however, Glen had something else to talk about.

"Did you know that Lynne had an affair?" he asked me.

If I have time to prepare, I can lie my way out of a paper

bag. But faced with a question requiring an immediate answer, I'm better off telling the truth. Any lie I tell would be so unconvincing it would make matters worse.

"Yes."

"Why didn't you tell me?" He was angry.

"Because Lynne asked me not to tell anyone?"

"I don't care what Lynne wanted. This was important. You should have told me."

"Why?"

"Why? Because I would have talked to her, I would have made her stop before it got this far."

Why is it that the men I know always think that they need to fix things? What's more, why do they think they can?

"Maybe it's none of your business," I said to my husband.

"Of course, it's my business. She's my sister."

"But that doesn't give you the right to know everything about her marriage."

"Are you siding with her in this?"

"Of course not. I'm just saying Lynne didn't want me to tell her what to do. She just wanted someone to share this with. I was a sounding board, that's all. And the truth is, I wouldn't have known what to say to her even if she had asked for advice. I don't know how things are between her and Brian. It's not my job to interfere or to offer advice. Giving advice would be dangerous when I don't know everything."

"She told him," Glen said. "He's devastated."

I laughed. Bad move, I know. But I could not picture a devastated Brian. An angry Brian, a pissed off Brian, yes. But not devastated. Something that unbelievable had to be comic.

"Don't confess," I had told Lynne. "Some secrets are best kept hidden," I had told her.

"If you had an affair, would you confess to me?" Glen asked.

Oh shit. The ground began to shift beneath my feet.

"It's a moot point," I said. "I am not having an affair."

"But would you tell me if you were?"

"Am I stupid?"

"What's that supposed to mean?"

"Just that a secret like that has the power to do immense harm. Confession might be good for the soul, but very bad for the marriage."

"I would want my wife to be honest with me. If I thought she wouldn't be, how could I ever trust her?"

"Is Brian glad that Lynne was honest with him?"

"No, of course not. How can he be glad?"

"So maybe if she had not told him, just carried on as she had decided to do, staying in the marriage, Brian's anger and hurt feelings could have been avoided. Sometimes it's kinder to lie. Or to not say anything at all."

"Is that the way you think, Sus? Because it's not the way I think and I feel as if I don't know you anymore."

"Glen, this is silly. This has nothing to do with us. Why are you so mad?"

This was getting out of control and far too close for comfort.

Glen threw his hands up in the air and walked out. I heard the truck start and leave the yard.

My husband didn't come home for supper that night and by eleven p.m., he still hadn't returned. If I had known he was out with friends, it would have been different. But

I didn't know where he was. And if I started phoning around, everyone would know that I didn't know where he was. I didn't want that.

I couldn't concentrate on anything. When I went to get a 7-Up out of the fridge, I selected a Coke instead and did not recognize the difference in taste till several gulps later. I wandered from room to room, looking out the windows for any sign of approaching headlights. I climbed the stairs to the attic, but could find nothing to hold my attention.

I did not lie to Glen. I am not having an affair. I have no plans to have an affair. I have never had an affair.

What I have had is a one-off. I can't even call it a one-night stand because there was very little standing involved and only a small fraction of a night.

Glen and his friend Scott were in the same grade. Their friendship was based on a shared interest in Star Wars and video games. I know him just because he comes from the area, but he left Manitoba to go to university and never returned. He was invited to our wedding, but didn't come. Didn't send a gift, either.

Almost two years ago, Scott's job in southern Ontario brought him to Winnipeg and he rented a car to come see his parents who still live here. He dropped in at the farm one evening after supper to see if Glen was around.

Had he called first, he might have saved himself the trip. It was early August, between haying and harvest, and Glen and some of his buddies had gone on a men-only fishing trip.

I remembered Scott as an extremely thin and gawky teenager. He had filled out nicely since then and the frizzy hair in his yearbook photo had been replaced by no hair at all. I did not know if it was early baldness or daily time spent with a shaver, but I approved. He had the skull for it.

I offered him a beer and we sat on the veranda and drank together. One beer became two. Dusk became evening. I lit some candles. When the mosquitoes became unbearable, we went into the house and settled on the couch.

I updated him on the farm. He told me about his job and the woman he had lived with for the past two years.

When we ran out of things to talk about, I let the beer do the talking.

"May I?" I asked, reaching out a hand towards his head.

"Go ahead."

His skin was smooth; I could find no traces of stubble. I swung one leg over, straddling him, and used both hands to shape the contours of his head. My thumbs found tiny areas of moistness behind his ears. I lowered his head against the modest cleavage that showed above my tank top.

"Come with me," I said, sliding off the couch and holding out my hand. I led him upstairs, stopping at the master bedroom to take a condom from the bedside table. Scott stood in the doorway, his eyes traveling the length of the room before resting on the bed.

"Not here," I said.

He followed me down the hall and into the bedroom that had years ago been Lynne's.

"Are you sure about this?" he asked.

"It's just sex," I said. It was a rationale I had been known to use before.

I helped Scott put on the condom, an activity that I had always found to be a turn on. Scott, however, did not seem to appreciate my efforts.

"I can do it myself, you know," he said and there was something in his voice that could have been embarrassment. "Never thought you couldn't," I said. "Just wanted to help. Do you want me to stop?"

"No."

That was as close as it came to bedroom foreplay, because no sooner was the condom in place, than Scott was on top of me. Up and down, in and out, an open mouth coming at my face like a fish at feeding time. And his ejaculation, while not premature, was a definite race to the finish, leaving me far behind and in the dust.

"That was great," he said, rolling off and flopping onto the barely disturbed bedspread.

"Un-hmm," I said.

He slept, mouth still open, for about half an hour while I lay awake wondering what the hell I had just done.

"Tell Glen I was sorry to miss him," Scott said later as he walked out to his rental.

"I'll do that," I said.

"How's he doing?" Glen asked when I told him about Scott's unexpected visit.

"He's bald," I said.

"Scott's bald? Really? Naturally or on purpose?"

"I never asked."

Scott told his parents that he had not been able to see Glen, but had learned from me all the family news. The condom did its job and my period arrived on time.

I told myself it was one of those occurrences that I could pack away in a box called "experience" and never examine again, except when I lifted the lid to put something else inside. But sometimes I was reminded that secrets have a way of seeping through the cracks of whatever is keeping them from the light.

The phone rang shortly after 12:30.

"Susan, do you want to come get Glen? He's had a lot to drink and he probably shouldn't be driving." It was Ben, a bachelor neighbour about four miles away.

"Sure, Ben," I said. "I'll be right there."

"Something going on?" Ben asked me when he answered the door. "Never seen Glen get so pissed."

"Just a bad day, I guess. Where is he?"

"In the living room."

My husband had reached near catatonic stage, head thrown back against the cushions of the couch. Ben helped me get him up and walked with us to the car. We put Glen in the car and I thanked Ben for calling me.

"We'll come get the truck in the morning," I said.

"He's going to be one sorry lad," Ben said.

Halfway home, Glen started fumbling with the seat belt.

"Gonna be sick," he said.

"Hang on." I stopped the car and reached over him to open the passenger door. At almost the same moment, he managed to unfasten the seat belt and leaned his head out the door. I withdrew my arm quickly.

When we got home, he refused my help. It was a slow and unsteady trip, but he made it to the kitchen and then slumped down on the floor. I could get him no further. I brought some blankets and a pillow; put the pillow under his head and the blankets over his body. Sam sniffed him and backed off. Tab jumped on Glen's stomach, did a couple of three hundred and sixty degree turns and eased into nap position. Glen didn't move.

"You may be sorry," I told the cat. Sam came with me to the bedroom.

"Girls against the guys tonight, I see," I said as she cuddled against me.

Glen had little to say for himself the next morning. I wanted to ask him about the drinking binge, but hesitated to bring up the fight. So I said nothing. We pretended nothing had happened. Neither one of us knew how to cross the distance between us. Nothing like this had ever happened to us before. Maybe he thought I was someone he didn't know, but I wasn't sure around him either.

I think Lynne was avoiding me. I didn't care. I felt relieved that the burden of sharing secrets was no longer on me. I wished I had never opened my mouth that evening in September and that I was just one of many to whom the current gossip was fodder for entertainment. It was easier when she was the daughter who could do no wrong. I knew how I felt about her then.

I felt used, as if I were a can she could empty her garbage into every once in a while and then walk away without a second thought. Or a sister confessor figure, although I had no power to grant forgiveness and had never offered any.

And yet at the same time I felt I had failed her somehow, as if somewhere in our coffee conversations there had been an opportunity for a connection that I had turned away from. Not a friendship. I can't see us ever being close friends. But a connection based on things we shared. It was complicated.

When Mom came home that weekend, I told her the news. Not the part about Glen spending the night on the kitchen floor; the part about Lynne telling Brian she had had an affair.

"I'm not surprised," Mom said.

If she was, she hid it well.

"Really?" I asked.

"It doesn't surprise me when anyone has an affair," she said. "Your dad would remind you that few animals are monogamous and that monogamy is a man-made rule, not a biological necessity."

That's true. I've heard him say it. Someday we'll ask our children, "Do you know what your grandfather would say?"

"Would you ever consider an affair?" I asked.

"I'm no different than anyone else," Mom said.

"I get the picture," I said. I didn't, not really, but I was afraid of what I might see if Mom decided to draw it for me.

~ SANDRA ~

I once asked my husband if he would ever leave me. Dave's answer, slow and thoughtful like most of what he says, was "Don't think so." When it was his turn to ask, I said no.

I wasn't lying. After all these years, I can't imagine a life that isn't here with him. And marriage can be such hard work that I don't want to start over again with anyone else. I don't have that much energy.

I was young when we got married, not in years

perhaps—I was twenty-six—but in what my grandparents always called "good old common sense". In those early months, I wrote incredibly bad poetry about my husband's hands:

> He has an artist's fingers
> in calloused disguise.
> His fingers feel the music of the soil.

He does have nice hands. The fingers are long and tapered, not meaty like his father's. His dad's hands are broad with sausage-like fingers. I call them farmer's hands. My dad has them, too. But Dave doesn't. It has nothing to do with art though. He's just a farmer with slender fingers.

The question we have never asked each other is whether either one of us would ever take a lover.

We have just arrived at the fairgrounds of a country fair competition. We set up our trailer, settle our heifer in the cattle barn, and after supper a group of us gather outside our trailers, drinking beer and coolers in the summer solstice twilight. I ask for a beer, and Greg Wright, a cattle breeder from another part of the province, brings one over. But instead of handing it directly to me, he slides the bottle lightly up the length of my left forearm. The bottle is cold and wet and it leaves a spider thin trail of liquid on my skin. Some men can make an invitation out of almost anything.

Then later that night I am restless and cannot sleep, so decide to walk over to the cattle barns to check on our heifer one last time. It is dark outside and the lights are on in the barn. Most of the animals are lying down in their stalls, although the occasional one still stands, tail swishing to ward off the flies. Fans are set up at the north and south entrances of the building.

Greg comes up to me at the stall where our heifer has settled for the night. We exchange cattlemen's pleasantries.

"Nice heifer you have there."

"What kind of feed ration do you have her on?"

"Is she a Goldsire daughter?"

"I'm gonna have one more beer before bed," he says. "Want to share?"

"Sure."

At the barn's centre an informal lounge has been arranged, hay bales serving as makeshift seating. Greg sits on one bale and I sit on another adjacent to his. We are within an arm's length of each other. I lift the beer bottle, and take a long, rather too quick, slug. Comes of being nervous, I suppose. I cough and he moves closer, an arm around me.

"Are you all right?"

"I'm fine," I croak. "It went down the wrong way."

"It happens," he says. He does not move away.

I take another drink and he takes the bottle from my hand, setting it down on the concrete floor. He traces my lips with fingers wet from the sweating glass and then leans over to lick the moisture away.

As I expect, he is a kickass kisser. His tongue is doing things that I never knew a tongue was capable of, but I sure like it. His hands begin to move and I like that, too. As we move closer, I drink in his smell, a potent mixture of barnyard and sweat with a very faint hint of aftershave that I don't recognize. I trace the shape of his upper body with my hands, coming to rest on the leather of his belt. In a few more seconds, I will head for the buckle.

But then a heifer in a stall at the south end of the barn moos and I open my eyes. I am sitting on a hay bale in the middle of a barn, surrounded on all sides by cattle. Call it an epiphany.

"This is just too biblical for my liking," I say.

"Huh?"

"The cattle are lowing," I say and move away from temptation.

Hours later, the kids and I are watching Dave compete in a purebred yearling heifer class. Greg is competing, too, although I always have a hard time thinking of him by his first name. Everyone calls him Mr. Wright. It's an old joke. He is, as our daughter Susan would say, a "hunk" and he has always known it.

We spend a lot of time throughout the year at fairs and competitions like these. Cattle are my husband's passion. The years have taken their toll, mind you—droughts, floods, bad prices, mad cow disease, and animal rightists. I'm not sure it's politically correct to be a farmer any longer. I think that's sad.

Dave loves his cows and so do the rest of us, although to a lesser degree. In our family the cattle come first, which is appropriate because they are, after all, our livelihood, but it has occasionally played havoc with family schedules. Just once it would be nice if a cow calved after the kids' hockey game, instead of just before or during it. It helps now that Jon, our seventeen-year-old son, has his drivers' license and can help with some of the chauffeuring duties.

And there Dave is, leading the red heifer around the

show ring, wearing blue jeans, a western shirt, and a peaked farmer's cap with *Twilight Simmentals* stitched across the front. Some of the entrants in this competition are wearing cowboy hats. My husband has never owned a cowboy hat. Cowboy hats have always turned me on but the boys and men who wear them are not, in my experience, good husband material. If you want steadiness without the thrills and spills, go for the farmer's cap.

We have spent hours and hours preparing our heifer for this show. We have shampooed her not once but several times; we have trimmed her hair and applied products to make the remaining hair shine and lie in the proper direction. We want to accentuate all her good points and camouflage the bad.

Judges look for signs that a female animal will be able to bear quality calves. They want a female that has pleasing dimensions. They want her to look feminine. She needs to have a well-developed and fault-free udder to feed her young efficiently. She needs a set of strong, sturdy hips for easy birthing. She needs well-formed legs, narrow front shoulders, and a straight back.

So simple really. Cows exist to make baby cows. Judging them on any other merits makes no sense. Which is not to say that people won't have their own preferences. Red cows. Brown cows. Black cows. White cows.

Personally I don't see what difference colour makes, but some people think it matters. There's a story about a producer who actually tried to dye his brown and white animals black before a big show. Cow colours go in and out of fashion like skirt lengths in another world. At that particular time, black was the colour of choice. Unfortunately for him it rained overnight, the barn roof leaked, and he woke the morning of the show to very streaky brown, black, and white cattle. The family got a five-year suspension from the show circuit. Quite the scandal. And like all scandals, there were those of us who enjoyed spreading the word.

Our animal is well-behaved and Dave has no trouble getting it to do whatever he asks. When the judge asks participants to stop, the young cow assumes the required pose with no prodding from my husband—legs positioned properly, back straight, head firmly forward.

"Atta girl," Jon says. He has taken an active role in working with Heidi, the name we have given the heifer. A maiden of the Alps. Her blood lines can be traced back to Switzerland, the birthplace of her breed.

What if women were put in a show ring, led around with a halter, and posed for the camera while a man judged us on our ability to make babies? Beauty pageants play the same role, of course, but they stop short of leading the contestants around on a leash.

I am basically boobless, although Dave, bless his heart, has never complained. In an udder competition, I would score embarrassingly low. I'd probably place fairly high on sturdiness and my hips would make me a good prospect. Legs? I hide mine in jeans. And the pretty face? Well, what's ordinary to one person is beautiful to another. Good thing, too.

I would not like to be placed at the bottom of the class. Imagine the humiliation. Like being the wallflower at a high-school dance without the option of hiding your shame in the girls' washroom.

The judge has started to line up the heifers. He first

selects the animals at the bottom of the class and works his way up to the top placements. We watch as one by one the owners bring their animals into line. It looks as if our animal will be in the top five.

It makes it to third place, directly behind Greg's animal. I can tell Dave is pleased by the glance he gives us.

I smile back at him, but I'm lost in a private daydream. Prize bull gets prize cow. It's a very straightforward story with no romantic complications. No pickup lines or flowers. Just sex.

And here's the other thing: once the act is done, the bull is removed from the story. The cow quite possibly will never again experience the pleasures of the flesh with this particular male. She is compliant and submissive that one time, but she doesn't have to live with him.

Her first time, she will probably be mated with an animal expected to sire lighter offspring. Giving birth for the first time is hard enough without having to push out the equivalent of a baby elephant. As she grows in maturity and size, she will be paired with larger males.

And since a cow's reproductive life can span more than a dozen years, while bulls often outlive their usefulness by the age of five, it's highly possible that at some point she will be paired with a young male the same age as her grandson. There's a May-December plotline for you.

There is movement in the show ring. The judge has been walking up and down the line, taking a closer look at the animals, leaning down to inspect teats, running a hand down a back leg.

Would I want a judge's eye on my cleavage or his hand

running down the length of my leg? It would depend on the judge.

The real judge, not the one in my daydreams, walks back towards my husband and speaks to him. Dave leads Heidi out of her third spot place and brings her up in front of Greg Wright's animal. The judge then spends several minutes comparing the hind quarters of our heifer and the animal in first place. No matter how pretty a heifer is, it's her business end that matters. At the judge's nod, Dave moves Heidi into first place.

Our children are excited, but cautious. They know that a judge can change his mind several times before being ready to live with his decision.

Living with a decision is not a bad definition of marriage, I think now, looking at my husband. When I got back to our camper last night, I did not go inside immediately. Instead I sat on one of the lawn chairs, leaned back, and looked at the stars. I picked one randomly and claimed it as mine. I made a choice, I guess you could say. Then I remembered the biblical star that shone its way to the barn. Enough with Christmas in June, I thought, and went to bed.

The judge's decision today is final. We are going to take home a trophy. Some prize money, too, although it will not cover the costs we have incurred. It's a lot about prestige, this business, not so much about making a living.

"Mom?" It's Sam, the thirteen-year-old.

"What?"

He mimes rather than speaks, cupping the fingers on his right hand as if he were holding something and pressing down with his forefinger.

"Oh, right," I answer and dig in my bag for the digital camera. I stand up and walk closer towards my husband and the breed association representative who is presenting my husband with a big red ribbon and a trophy. At first I can see both the first and second place heifers through my lens, with Mr. Wright's third-place arm intruding into the far corner. I zoom in, centre Dave and Heidi within the frame and press the shutter release.

~ SUSAN ~

Easter at Glen's parents was tense. Neither Lynne nor Brian had much to say. The presence of children and grandparents prevented any rehashing of Lynne's infidelity, but the air was heavy with what could not be said. The Triple As tried to make up for the unaccustomed silence by talking nonstop, interrupting each other, and tumbling over each other's words.

"I tried to look up pregnancy on the cow in the classroom, but my teacher said it wasn't appropriate," Alleyne said. "I don't know why; we're studying about the life cycles of animals and spring is the season of babies."

Grandpa Joe said that made perfect sense to him.

But then it turned out that the site Alleyne visited had more to do with fashionable ways to cover a baby bump than with biology or life science. The teacher had a point after all.

I was still wondering about the cow in the classroom. What was that?

"Computers on Wheels," Lynne said. "Instead of going to a computer lab, they bring the computers into the classroom. That way what used to be a computer lab can be used for a classroom."

"Auntie Susan, when is the baby coming?" six-year-old Adam asked.

"Just a few more weeks, I hope."

"Why do you say I hope?"

"Because I am ready for the baby to come out and I think the baby is, too. He kicks me all the time, like he's saying get a move on, lady."

"Is he kicking now?"

"Yes, he is."

"Can I feel him?"

"Sure you can." I guided Adam's hand over my belly. But the baby did not cooperate and Adam felt nothing.

"Maybe it's because of your shirt," he said. "Can you lift it up?"

"I guess." I pulled my T-shirt up over the huge mound that my stomach had become, exposing its tight surface to his view.

"Whoa," he said. "That's a big gut."

"Adam," his dad cautioned.

"It's OK. It is a big gut," I told the boy.

When he placed his warm hand on my belly, the baby responded with a kick.

"Wow," he said. "That's neat."

"Can I feel, too?" Brian asked. I hesitated, then said yes.

"I used to do this with Lynne," he said. He kneeled in front of me, placing both hands on my stomach, the fingers splayed out and fingertips pressing gently into flesh. When the baby kicked, he looked up at me and smiled. I smiled back, suddenly breathless.

That's why she married him, I thought. I hadn't realized until then.

"What are you two doing?" Glen asked, coming into the living room from the kitchen.

Brian withdrew his hands.

"Touching miracles," he said and walked out of the room.

"That was weird," Glen said.

"Yeah," I said. "Weird."

I thought it had been rather wonderful, too, but I didn't say so.

It's hard to say what will happen with Lynne and Brian, but if I were asked to place a bet, I'd wager on a stitched-up marriage. For the sake of the children. For the farm. For appearances. Who knows?

I went to see her on Easter Monday in the afternoon, before her kids came home from school. When she opened the door, I could tell she was surprised to see me.

"I've come for coffee," I said. "I hope that's OK."

"Of course it is, come in," she said. "Don't mind the mess, I've started spring housecleaning."

"You and I have a different definition of mess," I said, looking around the immaculate kitchen.

We talked about spring housecleaning and the baby and yesterday's Easter dinner, avoiding the affair as long as we could.

"I never felt guilty until it was all over. Is that strange?" Lynne said.

"I guess you were feeling other things," I said. "Like love, maybe?"

"No, I wasn't in love. Although maybe I was close, I

don't know. I think it was just so different. Usually I keep my feet on the ground. But now I was floating. I laughed at silly things. I did silly things."

"Sounds like you were having fun," I said.

"That's it exactly. I was having fun. For a few hours, I could pretend the real world didn't exist. It was like finding an oasis in the desert and spending time there."

"An oasis," I said. "Does that mean the real world is the desert?"

"No, of course not. But it does have deadlines and work and worrying about the kids. It's getting them on the school bus each morning before heading off to work, taking meals to the fields, manning the food booth at hockey tournaments, balancing the books at home and at work. There was none of that on the oasis. It was like a vacation.

"When I found out that Eric had left his wife, well, I did feel some guilt then. I thought I was the other woman. I had wrecked a marriage. And I thought, if Eric has made a choice, then maybe I should too. Even if that meant wrecking two marriages, not one. But a bigger part knew that it was way too soon for that. He didn't know me, not really. I had been pretending to be someone else. And I didn't know him either, obviously."

"And then he sent you the email," I said.

"Yes, and then he sent me that email," she said. "I should have guessed before then that there was something going on I didn't know about. We hadn't seen each other since he told me he left his wife. I was in the city a couple of times, but the timing was never right for him, he said. I never caught on. So when he finally told me the whole story, all I could do was cry. Well, you know … you saw me that day."

And then I got angry. I could have spit at him, if he'd been within spitting distance."

Even now, she could not bring herself to swear. Some things about Lynne would never change, I thought.

"I felt so humiliated. So stupid. I wasn't a main event; I was half-time entertainment," Lynne said. "And I never had a clue."

"I never told anyone," I said, which was true enough as far as it went. I did feel guilty about accidentally planting the seeds of gossip with my co-workers that day. That in itself was a form of betrayal.

"I know that," Lynne said. "It was Brian, after I told him. I think he told everyone who would listen. I didn't think he would do that. I knew that you would never tell. I was sorry that you found out, but I never worried about you telling. You're too much like Mom to do that."

"Me? Like your mom? Are you kidding?"

"No, I'm not kidding. You two are very much alike. Self-contained. You're more direct than she is but neither one of you is open."

"I'm sorry," I said, dropping the words into the silence that fell.

"What for?" she wanted to know.

"For being like your mother," I said. As a joke, it flopped badly. "I don't mean that," I added. Although maybe I did. "I guess I just meant that I'm sorry that it seems to have ended rather badly," I said.

"I know you told me to keep quiet about it, but I was reading this newspaper column. A woman asked the same question I was asking myself. Should I come clean or not? The answer was 'yes, you should. A secret like this is a tumour. Excise it before it becomes cancerous'. So that's what I did. The columnist's advice was like the straw that broke the camel's back, if you know what I mean. Brian was angry at first, then he got all whiny. How could I do that to him, he asked. It wasn't as if I consciously set out to hurt him. It wasn't about him at all. It was about me and what I wanted. Or what I thought I wanted. What I didn't know I wanted."

She paused.

"Brian actually wanted to know what Eric was like in bed. Can you believe that?" she asked.

"Yep," I said. "Boys have to know."

"I refused to tell Brian anything. Why should I? So he can tell all his friends? So he can feel sorry for himself some more? No. I hated him for being so whiny and I hated him for asking all these questions. But then he brought the kids into it. 'How could you do this to the kids?' he asked. And that got me where it hurt. Having an affair was like running away from home and now I was back again and Brian was reminding me that not only had I run away from him, but from our children as well. How could I have done that?"

Lynne looked straight at me when she asked the question, but I had no answer for her.

I'm not a little kid. I know that the world does not revolve around me. Life is not one big circle with me at its centre. It is many circles, encroaching on each other like in those Venn diagrams in high school math class. So many black lines, crossing through white space, until all you see is grey. I was lost in the grey of it all. The messiness. And I mean messiness by my definition, not Lynne's.

Jon, Andrea, and the boys dropped in after supper that same day to deliver a cradle that they were lending us. While the baby was small enough to fit inside, the cradle would go in our bedroom. Later we would move him to the crib in the yellow room.

"Want coffee?" I asked.

"Sure," my brother said.

"Decaf," my sister-in-law said.

The boys got juice.

"I suppose you have cows in your school, too?" I asked.

"Computers on wheels? Sure," Jon said. So then I had to explain why I wanted to know.

"Isn't it weird that you knew what I was talking about right away, because of an acronym that doesn't have anything to do with a real cow?" I asked. "I'm not even 30 yet and I feel like I've lost touch."

"No worries," Andrea said. "Once that baby is born, you'll be in the thick of things again."

# TEN

I am now fully dilated. Ten centimetres is the diameter of a soup can apparently, A regular can or one of the larger ones for chunky soup? I don't know. The math is beyond me. It's almost over, the nurse says. I'm not sure whether I believe her. It might be a con job, a way of leading me on, keeping me within sight of the finish line. You can do this. You're almost there.

My mother lied. She must have. There is absolutely no way that I could ever forget this.

Things that come in tens. The Ten Commandments. Ten Little Indians. Ten lords a-leaping. Ten fingers. Ten toes. Ten pin bowling. Cents in a dime. Years in a decade. Top Ten. Number 10 Downing Street. The perfect ten. Why wasn't I invited to the party ten doors down?

Just a week ago, I was trying to clean the bathtub. My belly made it impossible to reach the far side and I had to climb into the tub to get the job done.

"Can I have a maid?" I called out to Glen who was sitting at the kitchen table reading a paper.

"You've got it made?" he called back.

"No. I don't."

"What?"

"Never mind."

Mom had called to see how I was doing. A week into my maternity leave with another week remaining before my due date.

"I'm OK," I told her. "Want it to be over. I feel like a great big bloody cow."

"Just one more exam to write and I'll be home," she said. "Can't wait."

As it turned out, I did get a maid, after all. Joan offered to put in a couple of days washing walls and giving the main floor of the house a good spring cleaning. I wasn't all that concerned about the state of the walls, I confess. I certainly wasn't staying up nights worrying about it. The only reason I was losing any sleep these days was my frequent need to visit the bathroom during the night.

But I wasn't about to turn Joan down.

It wouldn't be correct to say that Joan attacks dirt, more that she forces it into submission. It retreated from her determination.

"Just leave me to it," she said, and I obeyed.

While she began the task of moving furniture away from the walls in the main living area, I withdrew to the kitchen and washed the breakfast dishes. I had brought up two pounds of hamburger the day before and left the meat to thaw overnight in the fridge. I began to make a batch of spaghetti sauce, first browning the hamburger, then adding the vegetable sauce I had made and frozen last fall. Tomatoes, carrots, onions, and peppers, simmering in a stew of Italian spices. It had made me nauseated last September. Now it smelled so good I couldn't wait for dinner. Comfort food.

## ~ JOAN ~

The wainscoting and plate rail that run the length of two walls in the dining room are a dark oak. Sandra has often told Susan that she should paint it white. It would open up the room, she says, and make it brighter. She is probably right, but I would miss the dark wood I lived with for so many years. Susan has so far held her mother off; Sandra would be here the next day with the paint, if given the slightest encouragement; that's the kind of person she is. But I think Susan is just as reluctant as I am to cover the wood's natural grain with white enamel. I am grateful for that, even though I remind myself that it would be none of my business. It is her house now. Well, hers and Glen's, but I would be surprised if my son showed any interest in its interior decoration.

The room is a mixture of "something old, something new:" heavy dark furniture left behind when Joe and I moved to town, splashes of colour here and there. Susan has married modern and antique in a surprisingly attractive union. Unfortunately all of it seems to be covered in pet hair as far as I can see.

Washing the walls in this house is not an easy task because of the twelve-foot ceilings. I used to complain when it was my job to do on a regular basis. But lately the larger the task the better. The more time it takes, the less time I have to think about other things.

So I shall spend a few days washing walls and windows in my old house, pretend that any resulting aches and pains are due to the size of the house and not to my own aging, and hold at bay as well as I can thoughts about the mess my daughter has got herself in.

People tell me that marriages fail all the time and the sky never falls because of it. I understand that men and women and their children, too, survive marital breakups and go on with their lives. But I don't want that for my children or for my grandchildren. If one more person tells me that it would not be the end of the world, I just may scream.

Lynne has risked everything she has for good sex. She's not the first; she won't be the last. When will women realize how foolish that is? It is easy to find good sex. Finding someone you can stand to live with is a lot harder.

If I'm honest with myself, though, I could have seen it coming, although I might have guessed that it would be Brian who would be caught straying first. He likes to flirt. They're both too caught up with "things," my daughter and son-in-law. Things like that big house and vehicles and hot-weather vacations.

Lynne has often told me that she is glad that Brian's family have never raised cattle because it ties you down so much. She doesn't know yet, or won't admit it if she does, that the desire to have the best of everything can tie you down, too. And there's a difference between being tied to living things—people, animals, plants—and inanimate objects. Living things give back. They grow under your care.

Only up to a point, of course. We might care about the land, but it does not care about us. We are irrelevant really. I understand my daughter's frustration with farm life because I have sometimes shared that frustration. Being a farmer is like getting on a train with designated stops at each season. A spring stop for seeding, summer for haying, autumn for the harvest, winter for the chores. You are carried along by the demands of the seasons and getting the train to stop for any other reason is difficult. Unless there is a breakdown and it's a side trip to town for repair parts. And the track is round; you do everything over and over again.

What Lynne has never understood is the pleasure that can be taken in the ride, and I'm not sure whether Brian does, either. Farming to both of them is a means to an end and that means is often unsatisfactory. They have bought into the "bigger is better" philosophy. I think, too, that Lynne seeks protection in her things. When she was a little girl, she was so easily upset by life: the calf that died, the dog that got run over, the clothes she could not buy because we could not afford them. Her possessions have become a kind of insurance against bad times.

I have always thought that Lynne and Brian made a good couple in many ways and I never worried about my daughter's choice. I knew she would be financially secure. But Lynne would be richer if she allowed some of her dad's quiet passion to show, not necessarily for farming, but for something she hasn't yet found. That passion exists; she's just very good at hiding it.

Neither of them told us about the affair; Joe heard it at the coffee shop in town.

"Is it true Lynne and Brian are breaking up?" someone asked him.

"Why would they break up?" Joe asked.

"I must have heard it wrong," the man said, obviously trying to backtrack and change the subject.

When I asked Lynne about it, she said, yes, they were having problems.

"I had an affair," she said.

Just like that, as if she were telling me that their car broke down or they had to purchase a new furnace.

We have always expected a certain standard of behaviour from our children and, with minor exceptions, they have lived up to those expectations. This was not minor. I'm sure Lynne could tell that from my facial expression, but her own matched mine in determination. Don't go there.

"I made a mistake and we're working it out," she said. "Don't be so judgemental, Mother."

I hate it when she calls me "mother." It means she is exasperated with me and my attitudes. She has often told me that I think in black and white with nothing in between, but that is not true. I was taught, however, that sticking to the rules helps you navigate through the greyness. You cannot get lost that way. It's like having a map to follow. I don't think that's a bad thing. Even having the map is no guarantee; it's damn hard to read in a fog.

Last night I dreamt that the children and I were visited

by three vagabonds, Gypsy-like in their dress and appearance. Joe was nowhere to be found and I was a younger version of myself, although old enough to have teenage children. The three visitors—two men and a woman—took us hostage in our own house, but we showed no resistance. They danced in their bright clothes and took us flying, their billowing sleeves serving as makeshift wings. It was magic, we thought. Even in a dream, the kids and I realized that people do not fly like birds.

One evening, the younger of the two men came to my bedroom and lay down beside me on the bed. Perhaps there was sexual activity, but I do not remember any. What I do remember—what I woke up still feeling—was an elastic longing stretched to its breaking point.

In my dream, the older man (who was not much older than my lover, but the acknowledged leader of the group) announced the next day that their visit with us was over. The girl was ready to leave, but the young man who had spent the night with me hung back.

He does not want to leave me, I thought. He wants me.

The emotions engendered by the dream lasted well into the morning until reason returned. It was only a dream, I told myself, and began to make lunch for Joe and myself. At my age, dreams are the only romance I can expect. Joe and I always had a good sex life, although never a noisy one. With first parents and then children and parents just down the hallway, we never felt alone. Our lovemaking became rather inventive as a result. How far could we go without waking the family? But when Joe's parents were gone and the kids were grown, we discovered we had forgotten how to make loud noises during sex. No matter.

Nothing says physical satisfaction has to be noisy, I suppose, and we were seldom unsatisfied.

Since Joe's stroke, however, things have changed. Lust has been replaced by affection and I mourn the absence of passion. It is a wonderful feeling to be told that you are wanted. At some point in my life, I will hear it for the last time. A depressing thought. I don't want to be old; maybe that is all it is. At some point in your life, everything is for the last time.

My daughter and I are not unlike each other, I suddenly think. Both yearning for things the way they were before life got in the way.

Standing on a step ladder to remove the drapes from the main window, I look out to the front lawn; an octagonal flower bed is emerging finally from its snow cover. Susan had added rocks and small shrubs to the display; in my day, it was planted to annuals. As if it was just last week, I can remember the first time the cows damaged that flowerbed. It happened more than once unfortunately, but the first time is clearer than any of the others. I drove home from town to find the carnage.

A fresh plop of cow dung steamed in the driveway. I parked the car over the offending pile and looked around the yard.

More cow pies dotted the yard, becoming shadows in the sickly green of the lawn. It had rained the evening before, an unwelcome rain in late June when we wanted to be out in the hayfields. We needed sunshine, not moisture.

Even more cloven hoof prints marked the lawn, pitting the surface like craters in a moon made of soft green cheese. The hooves had sunk inches deep into the ground and there had been a herd of hooves.

I placed the bag of groceries and our mail on the hood of the car and walked out onto the lawn, counting hoof prints as I went. I quit after twenty. I could also see the tread marks of an all-terrain vehicle. Someone, probably my husband Joe, had been trying to round up the cattle. To my way of thinking, he hadn't tried hard enough.

Tire treads and hoof prints were evidence that the animals had exited the yard through the ditch and then headed south down the road. If I had been paying more attention, I would have probably noticed the tracks on the road as I approached our yard. But I had been miles away, reliving that morning's conversation with our bank manager. Yes, I have a deposit. Yes, I realize we're overdrawn. Yes, I know our line of credit is up for review. Tell me something I don't know.

Tell me, for example, that things are going to turn around. Tell me that cattle prices are going to rebound. Tell me that it is going to quit raining and that our hay crop this year will be a bumper one.

We were not big farmers, but we were big enough that the workload was wearing us down. We were old enough to have parents who taught us that everything is possible if you work hard enough. But all the work in the world won't stop the rain from falling. Nor will it increase beef prices.

What really got me was when the bank manager started talking about our daughter in university. University is expensive, he said. Where did the money come for that?

Our daughter got a student loan, I said, because her parents could not afford tuition. She worked hard and received entrance scholarships. She had a part time job and worked hard at that, too.

"Good for her," he said.

I thought uneasily of the Canada Savings Bonds nestled in our safety deposit box. When the children were small, we made an annual fall trip to the bank to purchase bonds for their education. We gave our daughter her bonds when she moved to the city. It helped pay for her books. Not a large amount by any means. Was the manager suggesting that we should have given the money to the bank instead? Did he have his eyes on the remaining contents of the box? Wouldn't that be stealing from our kids?

But maybe we were the ones stealing from our kids. Maybe if we weren't trying so hard to keep this farm going, their futures would be better.

Rehashing it all was not doing me any good. But then neither was the view.

The octagonal flower bed at the front of the yard was a mangled mess. I had spent many winter hours planning this flower bed. There was more love in the planning than in the labour. In the middle of winter, dreaming of a perfect garden gives me purpose and pleasure. I seldom come anywhere close to making those dreams come true. I am good at dreaming, not gardening.

But that year I gave it my best. As soon as possible once the snow was gone, I made the flower bed ready. That meant coercing my husband into helping me. Together we cut the cedar tone edging into the desired lengths and made the eight-sided shape I had envisioned. We filled the inside with pail after pail of soil, adding home-grown fertilizer and store-bought nutrients as well. In my dreams, the bed contained ferns and hydrangeas. In reality, I planted petunias and marigolds. They are hardy plants—that's why I chose them over the more exotic stuff of my dreams—but they were not hardy enough to withstand this onslaught. The hoof marks in the flower bed overlaid each other in a frenzied pattern and would have been impossible to count had I made the effort. I didn't.

"Shit," I said.

Then I turned and faced the garden.

"Shit, shit, shit."

It wasn't enough. I wanted to stomp my feet and throw things like a two-year-old. I wanted to yell at Joe. I wanted him standing in front of me so that I could scream and stomp and wave my arms around. How did the cows get out? Why didn't you stop them? I wanted to spew vitriol at the cows, the stupid methane-gas producing animals.

But the yard was empty. Joe and his father were not there. Glen was in school. There were no cows. Even the dog was missing in action.

I wanted—no, I needed—to say something stronger than "shit."

But I don't say things like that. The excrement word, yes. I spread it around quite liberally. I am a farmer's wife. I know all about manure. It sneaks into my house on the bottoms of boots and attaches itself to the floorboards.

When Lynne was two, she learned her first swear word. From me. I forget what I was doing. Whatever it was, it obviously wasn't going well. Within minutes, she was imitating me. It came out "dit dit dit", but the intonation was unmistakable.

At the time I thanked God that she wasn't saying, "duck duck duck".

It would be appropriate now, though. Ducks with their webbed feet are made for rainy weather. I wish there had been ducks in my garden instead of cows.

The cows had fertilized the garden just as they had the lawn, but the worst damage came from the hoof prints. Some of the prints had water lying in them. Entire rows of corn, peas, and beans were obliterated; the fragile plants lay broken and tattered.

My kids used to sing a song about a bovine that leads her people out of serfdom with the aid of metal hardware. The chorus dips down into sonorous bass undertones with hints of Wild West menace. It always made us laugh.

Cows don't need guns. They come with hooves and those are weapon enough. I didn't see how my garden could survive those hooves and too much rain.

There's a story about a grain farmer in southern Manitoba who battled yearly with floods, droughts, infestations, and low prices. He bought a new combine and took it out in the fields for the first time. The ground was so wet and heavy that partway round the field, the combine broke in half. The farmer promptly went home and shot himself.

Good story, but it's not true. It's a rural myth, like an urban myth but with a combine.

We farmers seldom die with a big bang. Our end comes in bits and pieces, one season at a time. We live in next year country. Next year will be better. Sometimes it is. Sometimes it isn't.

The grocery bag had tipped over, spilling its contents over the car hood. A plastic tub of peanut butter had rolled off the hood and onto the ground. Without the weight of the bag to hold them down, envelopes had been picked up by the breeze and sent spiraling towards the house. I picked up one of them. It was our bank statement. Having talked to our bank manager just an hour before, I knew what the statement said. Unread, it still screamed of red ink. The deposit I had made that morning was only a Band-Aid; it could stem the flow for only so long.

"Do you think we grow money trees on this farm?"

My parents always said that whenever we asked for something. I said it to my own children. Money doesn't grow on trees. That's why we don't have an HD TV or a trampoline in the backyard or a car with a CD player. It's why we don't go on winter vacations. It's why your dad works 16-hour days and I have an off-farm job.

I wanted to say the same thing to the bank manager. Money doesn't grow on trees. Even if it did, trees don't grow without sun and rain in proper proportions. Just like crops.

But money is made from paper and paper is made from trees and trees grow in the soil. What fruit might this bank statement bear?

I took the envelope and carried it back to the garden, grabbing a hoe as I went. I frenziedly dug into the sodden ground, using a pre-existing hoof print as a guide. I stuck the envelope in the hole, covered it with mud and used the back of the hoe to pack it down. Let's see if money grows from that, I said to myself and laughed out loud. I felt triumphant and euphoric, like a magician hiding the rabbit that would later appear out of his hat.

But as suddenly as it had come, the euphoria evaporated.

This was our bank statement. How would I do a recon-ciliation if the statement was buried in the garden? I have always been meticulous, obsessive almost, about monthly bank reconciliations. And what if, someday, we were audited and we needed the cancelled cheques inside the envelope?

I could see the auditor sitting in front of me. It would be a man. A male auditor might be heartless, but a female could be mean. Even in my imagination, I didn't want to deal with a female auditor.

"Where are the missing cheques?" he would ask.

"I planted them," I would say, with a smile and a glance towards the garden.

"You what?"

"They never grew," I would sheepishly admit. "It was too wet."

The envelope was soggy and dirty, but had not been in the ground long enough to sustain any lasting damage. What the hell had I been thinking?

I had had enough. I would run away and join the circus. Although I did not know what use the circus would have for a middle-aged woman with absolutely no gymnastic skills, a fear of heights, a distrust of wild animals, and no beard to draw the curious.

I could man the admissions booth, I supposed. Or sell cotton candy. Or yell. Ladies and gentlemen, come and see the circus. I am good at yelling. If I had been here, instead of sitting as politely as possible in the bank man-ager's office, I could have been yelling at the cows. It might have done more good.

I gathered up the remainder of the mail and the jar of

peanut butter, refilled the grocery bag, and then headed into the house.

The telephone number was written on a magnet on the fridge door. Should I or shouldn't I? What would I say?

I dialed twice and hung up each time, then with a renewed resolve dialed once again, only to have to start over when I entered the number incorrectly. My hand tightened on the receiver as I finally heard the ringing tone.

"Farm and Rural Stress Line," a young-sounding female voice came through the wires and up against my ears.

I cleared my throat.

"Hello," I said, then stopped.

"Can I help you?" the voice asked.

"I don't know," I said.

"Can you tell me what happened?"

"The cows got in my garden," I said and burst into tears.

I hadn't realized I was crying now until I turned and saw Susan standing there with two cups of tea.

~ SUSAN ~

I had never seen Joan cry before. I might have even said that she wasn't capable of it. I did say it once to Glen and he defended his mother, admitting that she didn't often cry but that didn't mean she couldn't. If he'd been here now, it would have been an "I told you so" moment.

Setting the teacups down, I walked across the room and put my arms around her. She relaxed against me and I felt both compassion for this woman who was experiencing something that could bring her to tears, and confusion because I had no idea what that something could be.

It did not last long. Joan pulled herself away although her hands gripped my shoulders for a moment before she spoke.

"You brought tea," she said. "Thank you. I could use a break."

I brought the cups to the dining room table, pushing aside the pictures and decorations Joan had placed there when preparing to wash the walls. The cup I gave her was decorated with a crocus.

"That looks familiar," she said.

"It should. It was yours."

"Oh yes, that's right. I remember now. I won it as a door prize at a community tea. Not sure I ever used it though."

"Guess not, or you would never have left it here. Thank you for that, because I use it almost every day."

"That's right. You like crocuses, don't you? I'm glad you got it then."


"Don't push," the nurse tells me now. "I know you want to. But you mustn't. Not yet."

They wheel me into the delivery room and the doctor asks me to put my feet into the stirrups. My own doctor had talked about different positions; on my side, for example. Squatting like women in other cultures do. This guy is from the old school. I don't care. I'd attempt a head stand if he promised that would do the trick.

I push when the doctor tells me to and stop when he says. It seems to last forever. Carol told me this was the quickest part. She lied, too. Why does everyone lie?

"Think we are going to need the calf pullers?" Glen asks.

I stretch my neck to look up at him.

"Shut up," I say and I mean it.

"Sorry," he says. Perhaps he's worried I am going to swear at him again.

More pushing, bearing down, face screwed up in both determination and pain, and then suddenly it is over. There's a cessation of the pain and I feel the baby sliding out of me.

A boy. Eight pounds, four ounces. 21 inches long. He starts to cry and the nurse carries him away to do whatever it is they do with newborn babies. When she returns, she places the baby on my stomach with his head facing Glen and me.

I read somewhere that laying an infant on the mother's belly is an aid to the natural expulsion of the placenta. It promotes the contractions that are necessary for that expulsion. But calling them contractions is a misnomer. These contractions feel more like waves, an ebb and flow with purpose but no pain. I sense a final wave and hear a soft sound as the placenta drops into a receptacle on the floor between my legs. Detritus of a completed pregnancy.

The absence of pain is a kind of euphoria, a lightness that makes me feel as if my body with its suddenly flatter belly could float away.

My baby has very little hair, but what he has is dark like mine. His blue eyes may change colour, I have been told. All babies are born with blue eyes. He is looking at me.

Is this attachment, I wonder? This unbreakable eye-to-eye contact? You are my baby. Always my baby.

"Wanna know something?" Glen asks. "You know that woman next to you in the labour room?"

"How could I forget her?"

"Well, her husband went to have a nap in the visitor's lounge and the nurse woke him when it was time. Guess he passed out in the delivery room. Keeled right over, the nurse said."

I laughed.

"There is a God," I said.

"I phoned the grandparents."

"Mom, too?"

"Your mom first. She said to tell you she told you so. What's that about?"

"She said the baby was a boy."

The baby is sleeping, wrapped tightly in a blue receiving blanket. His fingers are curled into tiny loose fists.

"I have an idea for his name," Glen says.

"What?"

"I think we should call him Connor, what d'you think? It's like connecting the two families, yours and mine. The Connors and the Davidsons. Connor Davidson."

"It's good," I say. "Better than good. Why didn't we think of it before?"

"Who knows? It just came to me now."

"Can we call him Connor Lachlan?"

Glen laughs.

"Are you still on that? Yes, if you want."

"No, I don't want. I'm just jerking your chain. His second name will be Joseph. Connor for my family. Joseph for your dad. Davidson for everyone."

Glen is silent.

"Joseph means 'God will increase.' Very Biblical," I say.

"Don't tell Dad that."

"I won't. We're lucky it's a boy. We had nothing for a girl's name. Maybe that's why. Maybe subconsciously we knew it was a boy."

"Maybe."

I look down at the baby in my arms, touching his fragile head with my fingers.

"Welcome to the world, Connor Joseph Davidson," I say.

"He's perfect," Glen says.

"First and only perfect baby there ever was," I laugh.

No, not perfect. But he will do just fine, I think.

A nurse comes and takes Connor from my arms.

"Time for you to get some rest," she says.

Suddenly I realize how tired I am.

"I'll go," Glen says and leans over to kiss me. His lips are soft, his breath a little sour. I wonder what mine smells like and imagine it is even worse than his.

As he moves away, I see a tiny glass on the bedside table, more like a toothpick holder than a glass. In it are six crocus blossoms.

"Where did those come from?" I ask.

Glen laughs.

"They're the same ones I picked yesterday. I wrapped them in a wet Kleenex and brought them with us and asked the nurse to find something to put them in. You never noticed them till now?"

No, I hadn't. Too busy thinking about other things. I notice them now, though. Small purple petals in a small glass vase.

*Things that are small: The point at the end of a pen. The eye of a needle. Snowflakes. Raindrops. Grains of sand in an hourglass. Grains of wheat in a bin. Blades of grass in a pasture. A hummingbird's wings. A baby's fingers. Little things that fill the spaces between bigger things and hold them all in place. But which are which, because big and little don't always mean what you think they might. How to find room for them all. How to make them fit.*

"Too many puzzles," I think, not realizing that I have said the words out loud until Glen asks me to repeat myself.

"It was nothing," I say. "I'm rambling."

"Get some sleep," he says. "I'll see you later."

I realize I have forgotten something important.

"Thank you for the flowers," I say, but Glen is gone.

# ACKNOWLEDGEMENTS

I have many people to thank:

The staff at Turnstone Press for their support, encouragement, and patience with me.

Various instructors at Manitoba Writers' Guild workshops who worked with me on story manuscripts over the years.

The Manitoba Arts Council for grant funding to work on the stories and prepare a collection.

Sage Hill Writers' Retreat for giving me the opportunity to write without interruption on the stories and to share in the process with other writers. My Sage Hill Sisters Gwen Smid, Julianna McLean, Heather Haley, and Michelle Greysen for their advice and support. And instructor Terry Jordan, who continued his work with me during his stint as Writer in Residence at the Millennium Library in Winnipeg.

Friends and colleagues at the Manitoba Writers' Guild. Special thanks to Joanne Epp who took the time to read the manuscript in its early days.

The literary magazines *Prairie Fire, Room,* and *Cahoots* which published several of these stories before their conversion into book chapters.

My editor Kimmy Beach whose consistent message brought the novel to its present form, eliminating the unnecessary and polishing the bones.

My long time and dear friend Susan Ching, with my apologies for giving her name to a character who does not appreciate it.

And most of all, Kerry, Morgan, and Keaton, who have put up with me as I write and re-write and talk about writing. You may not always have all of my attention, but you always have all of my love.